DANGEROUS INTRIGUE

On the death of her father, Katherine Newcombe takes up a position in the household of a very respected family — but all is not as it seems in the Devonshire village. Miles Westcott, the schoolmaster, comes under attack when he investigates some of the strange happenings and Katherine herself is not left untouched by them. As Miles and Katherine draw closer together, the son of the local squire seems determined to force them apart, drawing them all into a dangerous situation.

KAREN ABBOTT

DANGEROUS INTRIGUE

Complete and Unabridged

LINFORD
Leicester

First published in Great Britain in 2004

First Linford Edition
published 2006

British Library CIP Data

Abbott, Karen
Dangerous intrigue.—Large print ed.—
Linford romance library
1. Love stories
2. Large type books
I. Title
823.9'14 [F]

ISBN 1–84617–142–3

Published by
F. A. Thorpe (Publishing)
Anstey, Leicestershire

Set by Words & Graphics Ltd.
Anstey, Leicestershire
Printed and bound in Great Britain by
T. J. International Ltd., Padstow, Cornwall

This book is printed on acid-free paper

1

Katherine Newcombe bade farewell to Dickon, a farmer's lad from her late father's parish of Payhembury in Devon, and stared about her with interest.

Compared to their village, Honiton was a busy, bustling place. Even though it was a dismal November day, smart horse-drawn carriages passed by with finely-dressed ladies and gentlemen seated within . . . and farm-carts bringing commodities to the market lumbered past at a slower pace.

Her dainty figure was enveloped in a black worsted cloak. The hem of her skirt, that peeped out below her cloak, was seen to be worn more for its warmth than as an item of fashion. Her dark hair, curling out from under her bonnet, framed an oval-shaped face and, although it was now set in solemn lines, a careful study of her features would entice the viewer to assume that a ready smile was more often to be found there.

Dickon had directed her through the stone archway that led into the cobbled courtyard of the inn, where she was now to await the Honiton-to-Sidmouth stagecoach, which would take her on the first stage of her journey, and she tentatively followed his directions.

A large notice on the wall of the inn attracted her attention. It read, **The Sidmouth-bound coach and four will depart from the courtyard of this inn at ten o'clock of the forenoon and at two o'clock of the afternoon. Gentlemen are advised to carry their firearms as a precaution against highwaymen and villains known to be in the vicinity. Gold, silver and all valuables are to be placed in the coach strongbox**.

Well, that didn't apply to her, Katherine decided. She had nothing to protect . . . apart from her workaday dress in her small handheld parcel and enough money to pay her fare to Ottersleigh that Reverend Cuming had kindly given her from the poor box.

Having lost her sole relative on her father's death six weeks ago, she had been compelled to seek some form of employment — yet what was she suited for? A governess? A servant?

The answer had come only yesterday.

The hand-written message was delivered to her via the services of the Royal Mail stagecoach from Honiton. It was from Reverend George Burrows, vicar at Ottersleigh, a village not far from Budleigh Salterton on Devonshire's south-eastern coast.

In it, the reverend gentleman offered to take Katherine into his household as a companion to his young wife who had been crippled in an accident and to help with the care of their four young children.

The message assured her that she would be welcome to take up the position as soon as arrangements could be made, due to his wife's unfortunate condition.

Katherine now moved closer to a small group of people who looked like prospective travellers. She positioned herself near to a woman of middle years, accompanied by a young woman of similar age to herself, Katherine guessed.

There, the similarity between them ended, for the other young lady was clothed in a cloak of deepest blue showing the hem of a paler blue dress edged with lace. The hood of the cloak was tossed back to display pale brown ringlets gathered high on her head. The girl's thin red lips pouted in a peevish manner as she impatiently tapped her foot on the cobbled ground.

'This really is too bad, Mamma!' she exclaimed loudly. 'Not only have we been subjected to a deplorably long wait for this coach but there will be half the population of Honiton trying to board it if it delays much longer! And most of them seem to be common riff-raff!' Her eyes slid sideways to rest scornfully on Katherine for the briefest of moments.

'Hush, dear! I know you are eager to start our journey . . . but people will hear you!' her mother whispered anxiously.

'And what if they do? It is to be hoped they have the manners not to listen to the conversations of their betters!' She imperiously twitched the fullness of her cloak away from Katherine's shabby, black one, continuing haughtily, 'I shall be thankful when Papa buys a carriage of our own! He keeps promising he will, now that our business is thriving! How will our wealthy neighbours ever deign to receive us if they know we haven't got our own carriage? They will think we are no better than common folk!'

Katherine raised an eyebrow at the ill manners of the girl and her lack of respect towards the other travellers, but before anyone had time to comment, the commanding sound of a coach-man's horn fluted through the air.

A frisson of excitement rippled through Katherine's body as the stage-coach, drawn by four chestnut horses, swept into the yard.

The whole place was suddenly a hive of activity. Grooms hurried out of the stables leading fresh horses; the coach-man urged everyone to, 'Stand back, there!' and porters appeared as if from nowhere, all eager to carry the luggage bags of the new arrivals into the inn.

'Excuse me, is this the coach to Sidmouth?' Katherine asked the coach-man.

'That's it, miss!'

She seated herself on the facing seat, by the window.

Two portly gentlemen followed Katherine into the coach, seating themselves next to her. They looked quite well-to-do, she thought, if the cut of their cloth was anything to go by. They wore warm cloaks with overlap-ping capes over their shoulders and tall beaver hats on their heads.

A young lad scrambled inside, sitting himself down next to the snooty young lady. He grinned at Katherine as the young lady swiftly moved nearer to her mother and tipped an audacious wink.

'Anyone got anything for the strong-box?' the coachman demanded looking at the passengers.

'No, thank you!' one of the men replied, unconsciously patting his bulging waist. 'I prefer to keep my valuables on me!' The tip of an ebony pistol was revealed as his cloak fell partly open. 'I defy any felon to take it from me!'

'You already have ours,' the older woman reminded him haughtily.

A few moments later, another ear-splitting blast sounded on the horn and the stagecoach jerked into motion. Out under the archway and on to Honiton's main street they lurched, the coachman keeping to a steady pace.

Katherine's face glowed. It felt so exciting! The only pity was the lack of visibility once they were clear of the town.

At last, they were on the open moors. It was slightly higher ground and the mist swirled more finely, showing it to be a ground or sea mist. Katherine fancied she could even see the faint glimmer of sunshine if she craned her neck against the window and peered up into the sky.

The man seated next to Katherine had an enormous ring on one finger. It had a dark green stone set in it and the gold setting was of an unusual design, like the claws of a wild animal. He noticed Katherine's glance and tapped it with his other hand.

'I see you admire my ring, miss,' he said conversationally. 'The stone is malachite. I mined it myself from Branscombe when I was but a lad. I always wear it. It reminds me from where I started!' He nodded sagely to the other passengers. 'It never does to forget your roots! Nothing to be ashamed about having worked your way up in life!'

Katherine wondered if he was referring to the young lady seated opposite. The girl's mother opened her mouth to speak but no-one was ever to know what she intended to say for at that moment a pistol shot rang out; the coach lurched violently from side to side and amidst a loud neighing of horses and shouted oaths from the male passengers, the coach was brought to a lumbering standstill.

Katherine pressed her face against the glass, trying to determine the cause of their unexpected stop.

She drew in her breath sharply.

A black-cloaked figure, his face masked, was seated astride a magnificent black stallion. The horse stepped delicately forward, the mist whirling about its head like wreaths of smoke.

Even as Katherine watched, the man leaned over from his saddle and took firm hold of the coach's leading horse's rein. In his other hand he held a pistol, aimed straight at the head of their driver.

Katherine swallowed.

'We seem to have been held up by a highwayman,' she said faintly.

The other two women started to scream hysterically, the elderly men blustered their outrage, the one with the pistol struggling to pull it out of his waistband; and the lad leaped to his feet reaching out for the door handle, inadvertently falling on top of the man with the pistol.

At that moment, the door was wrenched open and the terrified figure of their driver trembled before them.

'He . . . he says . . . you've . . . you've all to get out!' he stammered.

'I'll do no such thing!' the woman shrilled. 'Neither will my daughter! Drive on, man! Drive on!'

'I can't!' the driver said flatly. 'The man's holding my horses . . . and has got his pistol aimed at my head.'

Katherine's heart was pounding.

'I think we had better do as he says,' she suggested quietly.

The driver's trembling hands lowered

the step and he stood aside, allowing Katherine and the other two women to disembark with some degree of dignity. The passenger with the pistol was still struggling to release it from his waistband but was now in full sight of the highwayman. Another fired shot brought the passenger to a trembling halt.

'Throw it on to the ground!' the highwayman commanded, another pistol aimed straight at him. 'And you, coachman! Hold your horses!'

The highwayman adeptly exchanged the second-used pistol for another from his belt, revealing yet two more.

As the trembling passenger and coachman hastened to obey the order, Katherine observed their assailant. She grudgingly admitted to herself that there was a certain magnificence about him. He had superb control of his horse. Its coat gleamed like polished coal, as did the man's dark eyes glinting through the eyeholes of his mask.

His mouth was smiling — but it

wasn't a pleasant smile. There was a cruel twist to his lips and she sensed he was enjoying his victims' fear and his control over them.

'Please, sir, I beg of you, don't harm us!' the older woman pleaded, dropping to her knees.

She began to pull the rings off her fingers and held them out to him. Her daughter flung herself down beside her mother, sobbing wildly.

The highwayman's lips curled in derision. He detached a leather drawstring pouch from the pummel of his saddle and flung it to the lad.

'You, boy! Catch this! Collect their jewellery and money . . . and no tricks! I have my aim on you . . . and you others!' he ordered, swinging his other hand towards them as they huddled together.

He pointed the pistol at one of them. 'You! Get up on top and throw down the bags . . . all of them! And the strongbox! Toss your keys to him, the rest of you! Show everything!' He tossed another leather bag at the man. 'Put anything valuable in this!'

There was nothing any of them could do. They were held in the highwayman's power, as he towered above them on his mettlesome horse. It skittered nervously but the man's balance was perfect.

Whilst the man delving into the baggage hastily pulled out everyone's carefully packed belongings and thrust things of value into the bag, the lad held out the leather pouch to each passenger in turn, refusing to move on until everything had been dropped in.

He finally stood in front of Katherine. She met his eyes and shrugged her shoulders.

'I have nothing! No rings, nor trinkets; no money, except enough to get me from Sidmouth to Ottersleigh. If you take that, I shall have to beg for money to complete my journey.' She held her head erect. She would not plead; she had her pride, if nothing else.

'Stand aside, lad, and let me see the

13

maid!' the highwayman commanded.

Katherine straightened her posture and returned his gaze boldly. She was afraid . . . but, if she were killed, she knew she would be reunited with her beloved father and dear mamma. She defiantly tilted her chin a little higher.

'A winsome wench!' the highwayman declared. 'A kiss shall be your forfeit!'

His words took her by surprise and she felt a blush spread over her features. How dare he!

'My kisses are beyond price!' she retorted, surprised at her audacity.

'Aha! Spirited, too!' His eyes gleamed and his smile relaxed and broadened. He bowed from the waist. 'And I take none under duress!' he countered. 'Nonetheless, you will pay your due . . . some other time! Hand me the bag, boy! And you!' to the man.

He reached down for the bags, snatching them smoothly from the man and boy's grasp. At the same time, his horse reared, thrashing his forelegs high in the air.

The highwayman discharged one pistol into the air before laughing loudly and galloping swiftly away.

2

Everyone cowered backwards with gasps of alarm. The other girl screamed and fainted and Katherine moved over to help the girl's mother revive her and make sure her modesty was preserved as she was lifted back into the coach.

'Hurry, everyone! Hurry, before he returns! Let's be away from here!' the coachman urged.

'He'll not return,' one of the men countered flatly. 'He's got what he wanted! There's nothing of value left.'

With everyone back in the coach, the coachman lashed at his horses, spurring them into motion, tossing the passengers about uncomfortably.

The older woman wailed loudly, aimlessly flapping her hands now bare of rings.

'To see my only daughter lying prostrate on the ground, fearing her about to be violated . . . or worse! Oh, I feared she were dead! My poor Eliza! My smelling salts! Where are my smelling salts?'

'I was the one about to be violated, Mamma!' Eliza's voice shrilled, its power fully recovered. 'Oh, those terrible eyes! I do declare they shone like red lights! I believe he was the devil himself!'

'Don't talk nonsense, woman!' one of the men declared bluntly. 'He is as mortal as you and I and, one day, will swing for his misdeeds!'

'Oh, Mamma! Did you hear . . . ?'

'Hush, my pet! The man obviously has no sensitivity whatsoever! Oh, my darling Eliza! Your rings! My emeralds! My pearls! Oh, what will your papa say?'

'Be lucky if he gets the chance to say anything!' the man labelled as insensitive, muttered aloud. 'And naught but trinkets, the lot of them!'

'How dare you!'

'I deal in such, madam! My gold and

malachite signet ring is worth more than all of your trinkets put together! It's irreplaceable! Irreplaceable!'

The lad grinned at Katherine.

'I bet you're glad you 'ad nowt!'

Her smile of assent was wiped away by Eliza's, 'Yes, you two were lightly dealt with! It wouldn't surprise me if you were in league with him! I shall report you both to the authorities as soon as we arrive in Sidmouth!'

Katherine gaped at her.

'Don't be silly! He took nothing because I had nothing!'

She appealed to the two men.

'I assure you, I am recently bereaved and am on my way to be in service to Reverend Burrows, vicar of Ottersleigh. You may check it out, if you wish. I have nothing to fear!'

The girl narrowed her eyes.

'You must be guilty! You weren't afraid of him!'

'I was afraid!' Katherine admitted. 'But I was determined not to let it show!'

'Good for you, miss!' the lad praised. 'I weren't afraid, though! I think I'll be a highwayman when I grow up. Stand and deliver! Your money or your life!'

Eliza screamed again and both of the men bade the lad hold his tongue in his head.

He grinned unashamedly . . . then spoke to Katherine again.

'Did you say you're going to Ottersleigh, miss? I live there.'

'Really? What a coincidence! What's your name?'

'Ben Gillard, miss. I live with me ma and pa an' the rest o' me family at The Blue Anchor. We heard as how someone was coming to help the vicar's wife. She fell down the stairs and can't walk now.'

'Oh, poor woman! I hope I'll be of use to her. What is it like at Ottersleigh? Is it a pretty place?'

'It's all right,' he shrugged. 'I shan't stay there much longer, though. I'm goin' to sail the seven seas, as a pirate! Yoho, me hearties!'

Katherine smiled. 'Is that before or

after you're a highwayman?'

Ben grinned. 'It depends! Whichever comes first!'

The remainder of the journey was uneventful. They arrived in Sidmouth before noon and awaited the Sidmouth-to-Exmouth stagecoach that was due to depart at three hours after noon. Eliza and her mother were met by a middle-aged, overweight man of moderate means, who ushered them both into the parlour of the inn. Katherine made no move to follow them. She had had enough of their company.

The coachman hurried away to report the outrage to the proper authorities and the other passengers who had been robbed awaited their arrival.

Along with another five passengers, Katherine and Ben boarded the Sidmouth-to-Exmouth coach. At first, they travelled almost on the edge of the cliffs and Katherine was delighted to be able to see the sea.

'I've never seen the sea before!' she

mused, 'though I learned a little about the sea when I was at school.' She frowned a little. 'Shouldn't you be at school, Ben? It isn't holiday time, is it?'

Ben grimaced.

'Not likely! I'm thirteen, miss!' he boasted. 'Anyway, I was never there! I hated it! Old Petherick used his stick on me every time he saw me . . . so I stopped going!'

Katherine, whilst not liking his misuse of his teacher's name, was appalled that his education had been cut short by such means, though she had heard it was often the case that schoolmasters ruled with the rod.

'That's outrageous!' she declared. 'No-one can learn properly under such an attitude!'

'It don't worry me none, miss. I can read all I needs to an' I can count all t'barrels of ale we 'ave in t'cellar!'

Which was probably all he needed, Katherine reflected, as she sat back in her seat for a while.

It was mid-afternoon when the coach

pulled up at The Blue Anchor. Only Katherine and Ben alighted there. Ben swiftly disappeared around the rear of the inn.

Katherine looked about with interest. Apart from the inn, there was a watermill this side of the bridge and there were a few white-walled cottages along the road. In another direction, standing high above the trees, she could see a church spire. That must be where she was to go. More cottages lined the way, with small patches of grass and a few hardy flowers in front of them.

Katherine set off along the road. It was uphill and at last she turned in through two tall stone gateposts and walked up the short drive to the front door. A maid came to the door of the vicarage in answer to her knock and bade her step inside.

As Katherine looked around the spacious hallway, she felt slightly overawed. The walls were light and the floor was of polished wood. A beautiful chandelier of dangling crystals tinkled merrily in the moving air currents and a display of dried flowers sat upon a side table.

The maid disappeared and soon afterwards two young boys ran into the hall to stand and stare at her. Traces of jam around their mouths showed that they were in the process of having their tea. Slightly behind them, a pleasant-faced man with a harassed demeanour entered the hallway. He was carrying a baby and a young girl clung to his legs.

The man's hand was outstretched towards her.

'You must be Miss Newcombe. Welcome to our home! As you see, we were in the middle of tea, so do excuse us!'

'Oh, please don't apologise,' Katherine said, taking hold of his hand. 'It's my fault for coming so late. I didn't realise how long the journey would take and when the highwayman stopped us . . . '

'Highwayman?' the older boy echoed, his eyes gleaming with interest. 'Cor!

Did he kill anybody?'

'No! But it was quite a frightening experience!' Katherine assured him.

'I'm sure it was!' Reverend Burrows exclaimed. 'No more questions, boys! You must let Miss Newcombe recover from the ordeal! Come and meet my lady wife, Miss Newcombe. Phoebe, do leave go of my legs before I fall flat on my face! Boys, open the door for Miss Newcombe.'

Katherine was ushered into a pleasant sitting-room. It was a light, airy room, with pretty curtains at the windows and light covers on all the chairs.

Mrs Burrows reclined on a sofa. Wearing a pretty pale mauve dress, she looked very frail. Her chestnut hair was dressed in ringlets that hung in bunches at both sides of her head. She didn't look at all like a vicar's wife. She seemed so young and more like the lady of the manor, Katherine thought.

Smiling prettily, Mrs Burrows held out her hand to Katherine.

'Welcome to our home, Miss New-combe. We hope you will be very happy here, don't we, children?'

Katherine moved forward and it seemed appropriate to make a small curtsey as she replied, 'I'm sure I will, Mrs Burrows. I'll do my best, anyway.'

The four children were introduced. Henry and Zachary aged seven years and six years, were now busily wrestling on the rug in front of the fire and only paused long enough to say, 'How d'you do, Miss Newcombe?' on their father's orders.

Phoebe, aged five years, leaned against her mamma, her large brown eyes wide open. Baby Grace was being bounced up and down by Reverend Burrows and was squealing loudly with excitement.

'Now, children, run back to the kitchen to finish your tea and ask Martha to come to show Miss New-combe to her room,' Mrs Burrows said quietly. 'No, not Grace. She can stay here, can't you, baby? And, if you are all good children and get ready for bed nicely, you may all return and I'll tell you a story before you go to bed. Off you go, now.'

With the promise of a bedtime story, the three older children quickly scampered away and Mrs Burrows lay back against the cushions.

'They are good children . . . but so boisterous!' she said to Katherine, her voice now sounding weary. 'I love them so much and long to play with them but I can't . . . and that's that!' She smiled suddenly, its warmth lightening her face. 'And that's where you come in, dear. May we call you Katherine? It will make you so much more part of the family.'

'Yes, I'd like that.'

'Good. We'll talk about your duties tomorrow. I'm sure you've had enough excitement today. Ah, here's Martha to take you to your room. Since you've missed the children's tea-time, you must join George and me for dinner tonight. Come down whenever you're ready, dear.'

Katherine followed Martha out of the room and up the stairs to the landing, where they branched off to the left.

'Here's your room, miss. Master Henry and Zachary are next door that way and Miss Phoebe next door that way. Baby sleeps in here with you.'

Katherine looked around the room.

'It's lovely,' she praised.

The bed looked plump with thick feather mattress and pillow and a warm-looking eiderdown on top of woollen blankets. A lacy cover lay on top. Katherine felt sure it was made from Honiton lace, a well-known local produce, affordable only to the wealthy. There was also a side table by the bed and a tall wardrobe and chest of drawers — far too much cupboard space for her few clothes, that was for sure!

She felt completely bemused. Everything was so different from her former home and situation. Her own family had consisted solely of her parents and herself and, after her mamma's death, she and her father had lived alone. Katherine had kept the house clean and cooked their meals, making their meagre amount of money spread as far as she could. They had never had the luxury of a servant, never mind a cook, as the Burrows family did.

In way of making conversation, Katherine said, 'Mrs Burrows is a lovely lady, isn't she? She shows great courage. How dreadful to fall like that! I hope none of the children saw it happen.'

'No, they were in bed,' Martha assured her. 'Mrs Burrows went out for a walk like she often did. She loved walking out in the garden at night. It were such a shock when they brought her back to the house!' She drew her apron over her face. 'I'll never forget it! Never!'

Katherine was puzzled. 'Brought back to the house? I thought she fell down the stairs? Ben Gillard said . . . '

'Oh!' Martha's body stiffened and she dropped her apron. Her face was red and her eyes startled. 'Yes! Of course, miss!' she babbled. She flapped her arms in an agitated manner, backing towards the door. 'Don't tek no notice o' me, miss. I were thinkin' o' somethin' else! I mun go now! I'll . . . er . . . be in the kitchen if you needs me, miss!'

Katherine stared at the open doorway. Why should there be two tales about Mrs Burrow's fall?

After washing her hands and face and resting for a while looking out of the window, Katherine nervously made her way downstairs, arriving at the dining-room door just as Reverend Burrows was manoeuvring his wife's adapted chair on wheels through the doorway.

Mrs Burrows was wearing the prettiest dress Katherine had ever seen. It was made of pink silk and had a low-cut neckline that almost made Katherine gasp with surprise.

'You look lovely, Mrs Burrows,' she couldn't help saying.

Mrs Burrows smiled, her eyes twinkling.

'I expect you think I am dressed too finely for a vicar's wife,' she said in her soft musical voice. She turned and smiled up at her husband. 'George likes to see me looking pretty and, since my accident, this is one of the few ways I am able to do that . . . so you must forgive me if I seem too forward in my dress.'

Katherine felt embarrassed that her thoughts had been so easily discernible.

'I'm sorry,' she apologised. 'I've lived a very sheltered life and am learning so much now that I am in different surroundings. You have every right to look as lovely as you can . . . and to make your home lovely, too.'

She was relieved to discover the reason for the seeming extravagance in the vicarage. If she were confined to a life in captivity within a house, she, too, would want it to be as beautiful as possible.

The meal was splendidly cooked, from the delicate watercress soup, the roasted duck with orange sauce, roasted potatoes and steamed vegetables, to the frothy raspberry syllabub piped with cream.

'You must join us for dinner at least twice a week, Katherine. Mustn't she, George, dear?' Mrs Burrows said, as the meal drew to an end. 'We don't want your life to become a drudge, do we? And we must see about getting you some new gowns, dear. You must be adorned like the 'lilies of the field', as it says in the Good Book . . . not like the black crows in the treetops!'

Katherine blushed, partly in the shame at her dress being likened to a black crow and partly at the prospect of obtaining some pretty dresses.

'I retire early,' Mrs Burrows explained as Reverend Burrows drew her away from the dining-table. 'It is often a relief to be out of my chair and in my bed. There is no necessity for you to do likewise . . . but, as it has been an exciting day, maybe it would be the best thing for tonight.'

She wagged her finger playfully.

'Don't have any nightmares about highwaymen and other rogues. Martha will waken you in the morning and help you with the children. The three older ones go to the village school, so taking them there will be your first task.'

Katherine couldn't help thinking that there wouldn't be many employers who gave servants their orders in such a pleasant way.

By the time Martha knocked on her door the next morning, she had washed in the pretty rose-patterned bowl set upon the cupboard top and was dressed in her working frock. She self-consciously ran her hands over its creases, aware that it was much inferior to the one worn by Martha. Not that it had ever bothered her before! Oh, dear! Was she becoming worldly? She was once more aware of the differences between her previous state and her present one and felt somewhat perturbed.

She shook away her sombre thoughts and crossed the room to lift baby Grace out of her cot. The difference was probably because there was a woman in the house . . . a very feminine one at that!

'Come on,' she cooed to Grace, smiling readily. 'It's time to get up.'

The boys were full of high spirits at the breakfast table set in the nursery. Henry and Zachary started racing to see who could eat most bread in the shortest possible time.

'That's quite enough, boys!' Katherine exclaimed sharply. 'Get on with your breakfast quietly, please!' Maybe her upbringing had been stricter than in this household, but there were some standards she held firmly. She had almost finished spooning the porridge into Grace's continually opening mouth and she fixed her eyes upon the two culprits.

The boys paused from their activity, gaping in amazement.

'Martha lets us talk if we want to! Don't you, Martha?' Henry protested.

'I am not objecting to you talking . . . as long as you do it quietly!'

Katherine replied before Martha had time to respond to the appeal. 'It is the disgraceful way of pushing food into your mouths that I object to! Phoebe is younger than you but she is eating her food beautifully!'

'Martha says they are like little pigs!' Phoebe commented a little self-righteously.

'D'you mean like this?'

Zachary pushed yet more bread into his mouth and grinned round the table with bulging cheeks.

'Precisely that! Leave the table at once, Zachary!'

Zachary stared at her uncertainly.

'At once!' she repeated.

When he remained seated, Katherine turned to Martha, who was watching the scene with wide eyes, her cheeks pink with shock.

'Remove all the food that remains, Martha,' she asked pleasantly. 'Breakfast is over for today!'

'We've not finished!' Henry exploded.

'Yes, you have! Come along, Phoebe.

I'll get a cloth to wash Grace's fingers and face and you may wash your own hands in the bowl. And you, boys! Wipe your hands and faces and get ready for school!'

Katherine could hear them muttering in discontent as they somewhat resentfully washed their hands and then pulled on their boots.

'Do I take Grace with me?' Katherine asked Martha.

'No, miss. At least, I dun s'pose so! Me and Mrs Fairchild'll look after her. Unless you want me to come with you to show you the way,' she added hopefully, sensing that the episode wasn't yet over.

'I think I can manage, thank you, Martha,' Katherine said decisively.

She presented the three children to Reverend Burrows on their way past his study. He stopped his writing and patted each child on the head.

'That's good children!' he approved. 'Be sure to show Katherine the way. Off you go now. I'll see you at lunchtime.'

Katherine noticed the boys exchanging glances when she didn't immediately tell Reverend Burrows of their misbehaviour.

Thankfully, it was a dry morning. The early mist was slowly thinning and the sun was beginning to play among the tops of the trees.

'This way!' Henry called. 'Come on, Zac! Race you to the stile! And you, Phoebe!' He grabbed hold of Zachary's arm, preventing him pounding ahead and fixed his sister with a glare.

Phoebe looked slightly rebellious, obviously not wanting to race with her brothers.

'Come on! I'll hold your hand!' Katherine offered and set off after the two boys, pleased to be able to join their game and show them that she had a sense of fun. It was only when they emerged from the trees, crossed a narrow track and slithered down a steep bank to the river that she realised what the boys had done. They had led her in the wrong direction!

Henry was running towards a long, knotted rope dangling from the high branch of a tree by the water's edge.

'Henry! Don't you dare!' Katherine called out sharply.

Henry didn't even pause. He leaped at the rope and swung himself on to it out over the river.

'Whee!' he chortled gleefully, as he swung back and forth.

For a moment, Katherine feared he would let go of the rope whilst over the river . . . but he didn't . . . and, as the pendulum swing gradually slowed, she managed to grab hold of his legs and haul him to the ground.

'That is quite enough!' she said sternly. 'I shall decide on your punishment whilst you are at school, so don't think you will get away with it! Now, pick yourself up and lead us to your school with no more ado!'

'We're too late to go to school now! We'll be for it! We may as well play here until dinnertime and then go home. Martha sometimes lets us!'

Katherine recalled what Ben had said about the teacher's strict disciplinary tactics, but she wasn't going to ignore their naughtiness.

'Does she, indeed? Well, trouble or not, you're going to school . . . now! Or your father gets to know of this!'

Henry looked at Zachary. The implication that their father might not be told of their misdemeanour swayed his mind.

'All right, then!' He turned downstream. 'This is the quickest way, honestly!' he said as Katherine showed signs of doubt.

Katherine looked at Phoebe for verification and Phoebe nodded. She took hold of Katherine's hand again.

'Will I get into trouble, too?' she asked timidly. 'I didn't want to come but Henry said I had to.'

'We'll see about that,' Katherine temporised, feeling sorry for her. 'Let's catch up with the boys.'

The path along the river eventually led to a clearing and, to Katherine's relief, there was the village school, only a short distance from the church and vicarage.

Katherine felt slightly nervous herself. With Ben's comments about the teacher fresh in her mind, it was only the knowledge that she had to make a stand with the boys that induced her to boldly knock upon the classroom door and, on the command to enter, open the door and step inside.

About twenty pairs of eyes swung in their direction. Katherine felt her cheeks reddening.

'Good morning, Mister . . . ' What had Ben said the teacher was called?

'Yes?'

The schoolmaster's eyes moved from her face to regard severely the children by her side.

To Katherine's amazement, the teacher wasn't old at all! Well, not in her eyes! Maybe to a child of Ben's age he might seem old. He seemed barely in his mid-twenties, she guessed. He had dark brown hair, worn rather shorter than she was used to seeing. It was brushed rather carelessly forward, framing his pleasant, if stern face. He was quite good-looking, she decided with a shock, especially his dark brown eyes, which were visibly softening in their expression as he regarded her.

Her heart seemed to stop beating as she found her eyes were rivetted upon his face. She felt that she wanted to glide forward and be enveloped in his arms and feel the softness of his lips upon . . .

Her cheeks suddenly went hot. Whatever was she thinking of? This man was used to wielding a cane with ferocious delight! Deciding to concentrate on the severity of his expression rather than the contours of his face, she took a deep breath to steady her voice and began again.

'I'm sorry we are late, Mr . . . er . . . ' Oh, dear! Why hadn't she asked Henry what their teacher was called! 'It's my first day with the Burrows family. It was slightly misty and we . . . er . . . got lost.'

The young man raised his eyebrows.

'Yes, I can quite see how easy it must be to get lost in the mist between the vicarage and the school!' he said dryly.

There were some titters among the scholars . . . but these were quelled with a stern glance from the teacher. He then focussed on Henry and Zachary.

'You two! Stand by my desk! I will deal with you in a moment! Sit down in your place, Phoebe. The rest of you, copy the writing from the board on to your slates.'

Katherine caught sight of the long stick that was leaning against the wall by the chalkboard.

'Don't you dare cane them!' she warned boldly. 'Beating a child is no way to control him!'

The children, seated in neat rows, were open-mouthed and wide-eyed. Katherine felt herself blushing again but she faced him bravely. Her father had never condoned corporal punishment at his village school and she whole-heartedly agreed with him!

The teacher glared at her and then turned to his class.

'Eyes down on your work! Not a sound whilst I am out of the room!'

He gripped hold of Katherine's arm above her elbow, turning her towards the door.

'Step outside, if you please, Miss . . . ' he said firmly.

Unable to pull her arm free, Katherine had no option but to obey . . . but she felt furious. How dare he! If he could treat her like this, how much worse must he be with the children?

'Release me, sir!' she exclaimed. 'You have no right . . . '

'And you have no right to disturb my class or challenge my authority and discipline!'

'Indeed?'

She drew herself as tall as she was able.

'Only a coward would cane a

defenceless child!' she declared haughtily.

'Really? I am glad you think so
. . . for that is my sentiment also,' he
agreed whole-heartedly.

3

Katherine paused. 'You do? Then why on earth are we having this ridiculous argument?'

'I would like to hear the answer to that myself, Miss . . . '

She tried to remain aloof but she found it very difficult, since her eyes kept wandering to his lips, wondering if they were as soft and velvety as they seemed . . . and if that small curl of hair that hung over his forehead would twist around her finger before it flew back into its place. She swallowed hard.

'I have heard, on the best of authority, that you have frequently caned boys for mere misdemeanours and have even driven boys away from their schooling by such action!'

'Indeed! And may I ask what is the source of this best of authority?'

'Oh!' Katherine swallowed, suddenly

wondering just how good an authority Ben might be. 'A boy who used to come here . . . until he could bear to come no more!'

'And how old might this boy be?'

'Thirteen. A boy who . . . '

'I began to teach here only this year!'

Oh, dear! It didn't take much mathematical knowledge to calculate that Ben must have left school three or four years ago. Katherine's hands flew to cover her cheeks. What had she done! The poor man! She had vilified him for no just reason!

'Then you aren't Mr Pe . . . Pev . . . ?'

'Mr Petherick? No, I am not.'

Numbly, she raised her eyes to meet his. To her amazement he was smiling at her. She looked away in confusion.

She swallowed hard again.

'I think I owe you an apology, Mr . . . '

'Miles Westcott. And you are?'

'Katherine Newcombe. I am . . . er . . . newly arrived here. I'm sorry,' she mumbled. 'I didn't know. Oh, dear, you must think me very ill-mannered!'

His expression softened.

'I think you are a very kind-hearted person . . . though somewhat impetuous in nature,' he remarked candidly.

Katherine nodded, though her cheeks were still burning.

'Papa used to warn me about rushing in where angels fear to tread!' she admitted ruefully. She sighed sadly. 'I have forgotten so soon.'

They smiled at each other for a moment, neither seeming to want to be the one to turn away first. It was the schoolmaster who broke his gaze.

'I must beg you to excuse me, Miss Newcombe. I can't expect my young scallywags to remain quiet for much longer.' He cocked an ear towards his classroom door, from behind which a growing murmur was building up.

'Yes, I understand.' How embarrassing it must be for him! Would he ever find it in his heart to forgive her? 'Good day, Mr Westcott.'

With a quick smile and the barest of

nods, Mr Westcott strode back into his classroom, once more closing the door as Katherine heard his voice say, 'Stand to attention, everyone!'

With a lingering look at the closed door, Katherine turned and slowly made her way back to the vicarage, her mind dwelling on the recent encounter. If only she had met Mr Westcott in different circumstances, she felt sure they might have become friends! As it was, he most likely thought she was an empty-headed maiden, not worthy of his friendship . . . in spite of his kind words that he had spoken to put her at her ease.

What had possessed her to speak so forthrightly to him? And in front of the whole school! Even if her accusation had been true, it was entirely the wrong way to have gone about it!

She was almost running by the time she re-entered the vicarage, this time through the rear door into the kitchen.

'Lawk a' me! What ails thee, child?' Alice Fairchild exclaimed, seeing

47

Katherine's red face and bright eyes. 'Be there a fire or sommat?'

'Oh, no, no! I thought I might be late back! I'm sorry I took so long!' Katherine hastened to apologise. 'It's such a nice day out there . . . and . . . She faltered, deciding she may as well admit to have been the butt of Henry's mischief. 'I'm afraid I allowed Henry to lure me into a rather roundabout way to the school, making us late.'

'Aye, that sounds like master Henry, a'right! Don't ye worry none! You'll get the hang of him, I don't doubt. Now sit ye down and I'll make ye some toast. I don't suppose you had much to eat with the children, did you?'

Katherine laughed, relieved to have the incident made so little of. She could only hope that Mr Westcott was of similar mind.

Katherine would have been surprised to learn that Miles Westcott's thoughts were in similar vein.

He had swiftly brought his class back under control and had set them chanting their times tables . . . but his mind was far away, following the soberly dressed figure of the prettiest girl he had seen since he came to Ottersleigh. Her ability to laugh at her own impetuosity brought a smile to his face as he recalled her reminiscent phrase of, 'fools rush in.'

He eventually forced himself to concentrate on the morning's lessons, consoling himself that he would, no doubt, see the delightful Miss New-combe again before nightfall.

★　★　★

'So, Henry! What have you to say for yourself?'

Katherine faced the seven-year old sternly, determined to impress upon him that his behaviour that morning that been far from exemplary.

Henry scuffed the toe of his right boot against the floor and then absently rubbed it up and down over his left ankle.

'I'm sorry, I s'pose.' He grinned. 'You didn't half tell old Waistcoat what to do with his stick! He's put it in his cupboard out of sight! Not that he's ever used it! Not like old Candlewick did!'

Katherine strove hard to keep her face straight.

'Your teacher's name is Mr Westcott, Henry! I will have no disrespect against your teachers, past or present! Is that understood?'

Henry sighed but managed to look a little abashed. 'Yes.' He then looked at her coyly. 'It doesn't mean I'm going to turn into some sort of angel, though!'

Over the next few days, Katherine settled swiftly into her new life. Mrs Burrows, Sarah, as she asked Katherine to call her, was not a demanding person. Even in her crippled state, she was full of fun and life and seemed to want Katherine to share it with her.

'It's as if God had given me a second chance at life,' she confessed to Katherine one morning. 'As soon as we heard about your tragic circumstances, having lost not only both your parents but also your home and livelihood, I said to George, 'We can help that girl! Just think what would happen to our children in similar circumstances!' Of course, he told me not to think of such things — but he agreed that I needed help around the house.'

'You're being very kind to me. I'll never be able to repay you.'

'We don't want repaying . . . we have enough of everything. We just want you to be happy here. You are happy, aren't you?'

'Oh, yes! It all seems like a dream!'

Katherine's face sobered a little as she thought of all that Sarah had already given her. Six new dresses were on order; a lighter-weight blue cloak and a number of pairs of shoes and boots — far more than she had ever owned in her entire life! How could they afford it on a parson's salary?

'What is it, Katherine, dear? You

seem anxious about something! Do tell me.'

'Well, it just seems . . . you have a lot more than we ever had at home. Not that we were ever in want!' she hastened to add. 'My father was a wonderful man and he never grumbled or bemoaned our poor state but we never had anything like this!' She spread her hands, indicating the lovely décor and furnishings of the parlour — and, indeed the rest of the house.

Sarah smiled. 'Let us just say that God is good,' she remarked enigmatically. 'He has placed us here in this village and our parishioners share whatever comes their way.'

'Their tithes, do you mean?' Katherine asked, still puzzled.

'Yes, if you like . . . but I think they give more than a tenth, especially since my accident. We pondered over it what to do,' she confessed, 'and decided to accept their gifts as inspired by God and to give out from them ourselves, passing on the bounty. Were we right, do you think?'

Katherine smiled at the earnestness of Sarah's expression.

'Yes, I'm sure you must be,' she replied, finding it difficult to imagine Sarah doing anything that was wrong. 'And I will pass it on by giving you and your family my whole-hearted support!'

The first time she had taken the children to school after that first morning, she made sure that they were in plenty of time and, after ushering her charges into the playground, she hastily made her retreat, not wanting to run the risk of meeting Mr Westcott again . . . at least, not quite so soon. Maybe, once he had had time to forget her impulsive and misinformed accusation, he might view her with charitable forgiveness.

However, on Friday afternoon, as she waited under the shelter of the trees beyond the playground since it was pouring with rain, she was dismayed to see only Henry and Zachary running towards her.

'Feeble Phoebe's had to stay in to finish her work!' Henry chortled, glad that someone other than himself was in bother. 'Mr Waistcoat . . . ' His face fell as he noticed Katherine's stern expression. 'I mean Westcott . . . said to tell you to collect her from the classroom! Can me and Zac run home?'

'What? Oh, yes, I suppose you'd better do that.'

Oh dear! Katherine couldn't imagine little Phoebe in trouble!

She needn't have worried. Mr Westcott looked up smiling as she opened the door in response to his, 'Come in!' and Phoebe herself seemed well-content.

Mr Westcott rose to greet Katherine, holding out his hand.

'Miss Newcombe! How good of you to stop by! No, no . . . don't look so anxious! I merely wanted to point out to you how delightfully Phoebe has drawn the nature specimen. Now that she has finished it, I will mount it and display it upon the classroom wall. If you would tell Reverend Burrows and his wife, I am sure they will be pleased!'

Phoebe's face was pink with pleasure at the praise.

Katherine smiled her delight, her own cheeks glowing as she read the open admiration on the teacher's face.

'Thank you for allowing me to see Phoebe's picture. It's truly delightful. I must make sure Mrs Burrows gets an opportunity to see it.'

They smiled at each other, as they had on the previous occasion of their meeting. This time it was Katherine who broke away.

'Well, Phoebe, we must be going home. Mrs Fairchild will have our tea ready, so we mustn't delay. It will be getting quite dark out there.' She held out her hand to Mr Westcott. 'Thank you, once again, Mr Westcott.'

Mr Westcott clasped her hand in his, his dark chocolate-coloured eyes smiling into hers. His touch thrilled her.

'I . . . er . . . wondered if we might walk along by the river tomorrow,' Mr Westcott said hesitantly. 'That is . . . if you have any free time?'

'Oh! That would be delightful! But I'm not sure. I'll probably have the children to mind . . . all day, I expect.' She smiled at his evident disappointment, a warm feeling of happiness spiralling through her, making her add, 'But, maybe, if the day is fine, I could take them down by the river say, after lunch, for an hour or so.'

Mr Westcott's face shone again.

'Excellent! Until tomorrow, then, Miss Newcombe.'

Unsure how to explain the arranged meeting, she decided not to mention it in advance . . . just in case nothing came of it. Mr Westcott might change his mind before tomorrow and she didn't want to appear foolish.

As it happened, the meeting was doomed for quite a different reason. As soon as Katherine and Phoebe had taken off their wet cloaks, Alice passed on a message from Mrs Burrows requesting Katherine to go to the parlour as soon as she came home. After assuring Alice and Martha that Phoebe hadn't been in trouble . . . to the contrary, had been worthy of praise . . . she made her way swiftly to the parlour, hoping no-one had mis-reported her private meeting with the schoolmaster.

Sarah's face brightened immediately Katherine entered the parlour. She clasped her hands together in delight.

'You'll never guess what I am about to tell you, Katherine, dear . . . so I won't tease you! You have been invited to accompany George and me to the manor tomorrow evening to attend the annual ball! Isn't that delightful? As soon as Lady Densham heard of you, she implored me to bring you along! You did say your father didn't want you to go into mourning, didn't you? I thought so. What a good thing your new gowns are on order! Mrs Toms is coming tomorrow afternoon to do the final fitting and she's promised to stay on and finish at least one of the garments.'

Katherine's initial pleasure was dampened by the final sentence. Her face fell.

'Oh! I had thought to take the children down to the river tomorrow afternoon.'

'Never mind. George can take them.'

And, not wanting to make more of her arrangement to see Mr Westcott by the river than was meant, Katherine had to hope that he would assume by Reverend Burrow's presence with the children that she had a valid reason for failing to keep the appointment.

Her disappointment was quickly dispelled by the pleasure of trying on three pretty day dresses in winter-weight cloth, one walking-out outfit and two elegant gowns for evening wear. One was in pale blue satin, with a gauze overskirt embroidered in blue flowers; and the other was white muslin. Its small puff sleeves and low neckline revealed the delicate, milky white skin of her neck, arms and shoulders.

Katherine gasped with a mixture of delight and shock when, wearing the white muslin, she viewed herself in the long mirror in Sarah's private bedroom on the ground floor where the fitting was taking place. Never had Katherine seen so much of her flesh, since the only mirror they had had at home was a small round one in their hallway to check that they were tidy before venturing outdoors.

'You look lovely, Katherine,' Sarah said.

'I'm only a servant! I cannot go dressed like this, Sarah!'

'You will look just like everyone else, Katherine . . . except you will outshine them all with your beauty! Trust me! And, dear Katherine, never, never regard yourself as a servant. Neither I nor George regard you in that way.'

Katherine felt tears prick at her eyes. They were so kind to her! She touched her cheek wistfully.

'Am I really beautiful?' she asked. It

had never occurred to her to wonder.

'Yes . . . and when I have dressed your hair, you will be even more so!'

Sarah read the doubt on Katherine's face. She reached out her hand towards Katherine, drawing her away from the ministrations of the dressmaker.

'Come here, my dear.'

Katherine drew close to her and Sarah took hold of her hand. Her eyes had lost their gaiety and had taken on an air of wistful pleading.

'Let me do this, Katherine. My daughters are very young. It will be twelve years or more before Phoebe will be old enough for me to launch her, as it were . . . and, who knows, I may not live that long. No, no! Do not pity me!' as Katherine's expression changed to alarm at her words. 'The Lord has now given me grace to enjoy each day as it comes.

'Now, promise me that you will wear one of these lovely gowns tonight and enjoy the ball. I have described your situation as being our ward, put into our care by the bishop and that, whilst you are also here as my companion and to help me with the children, you are in no way a servant. Lady Densham was gracious enough to accept you as such . . . and where she leads, others will follow.'

Their delightful couple of hours in feminine pleasure were brought to an end by the arrival home of the children and Reverend Burrows. They had taken off their muddy boots but nothing else and both Sarah and Katherine shrieked when they burst into the room looking like gipsy children.

'Stay there! Come no farther!' Sarah bade them, her hand outstretched, bringing their charge to a standstill.

'Mamma! Mamma! We've had a wonderful time!' Phoebe cried out in excitement.

'We're building a raft!' Henry said.

'With Mr Westcott! He says it's our own pro . . . pro . . . ' Zachary struggled.

'Project, stupid! He's going to get

proper materials!' Henry added. 'And we're to help him every Saturday!'

'Children! Back to the kitchen!' George's voice came over their heads. He nodded his head in approval of what the boys were saying.

'Yes, Mr Westcott seems to have a remarkable rapport with our boys, Sarah . . . and Phoebe also . . . for all some parents are saying he is far too lenient and lacking in discipline. He has instilled quite a lot of mathematical and scientific knowledge into their heads this afternoon . . . and I don't suppose any of them are aware of it!'

Katherine was pleased to hear Mr Westcott being praised. She felt a wave of reflected glory washing over her on account of her hoped-for association with him . . . a very satisfactory feeling!

4

At seven o'clock they were ready to depart. The children had been bathed and put to bed with firm orders to stay there ringing in their ears — with the added promise of permission for further Saturday raft-building expeditions if a good report was given of them!

Alice and Martha were left in charge.

Sarah's chair was not being taken to the manor house. They were arriving early so that George could carry his wife into the ballroom and seat her upon a suitable, comfortable chaise-longue.

The vicarage, which in Katherine's eyes was full of splendour, faded into insignificance when compared to the sumptuous wealth displayed in Ottersleigh Manor House.

The entrance hall was huge. A polished oak floor reflected the glittering lights from the magnificent chandelier that hung overhead. Small, spindle-legged tables held fabulous displays of hot-house blooms, adding a fine array of colour to the hall. They drew Katherine's gaze to the wide-open double doors leading into an ante-room tastefully decorated in cream and beige wall hangings and full-length mirrors, making the room seem twice as large as it really was.

Not for the first time Katherine wondered what it was about this village that set it apart from others. Cornwall was renowned for its tin mines. Did Ottersleigh sit upon a goldmine? Or silver? Or diamonds?

Katherine felt superfluous to requirements and wandered from one spectacular ornament or painting to another, her feet taking her in a circular route through a succession of rooms.

She was surprised to find herself back in the entrance hall. A number of guests were now arriving. Smartly-dressed servants in gold and silver livery divested them of cloak and wraps and a distinguished-looking gentleman took a card from each party and announced their names to a handsome couple of middle years who were standing at the foot of the grand staircase that curved its way down from the upper floor. Katherine supposed them to be Lord William Densham and his wife, Lady Clara.

A movement on the staircase drew her eyes upwards. The silk-clad figure of a young man came fully into view. His coat and breeches were of deepest red; his calves were encased in close-fitting cream silk stockings and golden buckles adorned each shoe. A froth of fine lace dangled from both wrists and a veritable waterfall of lace cascaded from his throat.

Katherine caught her breath as her gaze came to rest on his face. He was a handsome man, whose hair was as black as jet and, in this light, his eyes also seemed to gleam as black as coal.

Her gasp caught the man's attention and he paused partway down the stair-case, his eyes holding hers. Katherine sensed rather than heard the whistled intake of his breath. Such blatant admiration shone from his eyes that she turned and looked over her shoulder to see at whom he was gazing but no-one was there.

She looked back again. His sensual mouth held a smile, a strange smile, Katherine thought, unable to put into words exactly what she felt. It portrayed neither warmth nor welcome, more of possession, or intent of such. She felt a shiver run down her spine and made to turn away to hasten back to Sarah's side but the man called out, 'Wait!'

More used to obeying than not, Katherine paused — though still poised for flight.

The man reached her side and towered over her.

Though intimidated by his height and grandeur, Katherine lifted her face to meet his gaze. Why should she fear him? She was an invited guest and had done no wrong.

The man took hold of her hand and

swept into an extravagant low bow, bringing her fingers to his lips as he straightened.

'I'm afraid I missed your introduction,' he said, his eyes boring into hers. 'And yet, I feel we have met before, have we not?'

Katherine was startled both by his obvious admiration of her and his boldness of address. She might be a country parson's naïve daughter but she knew there were social conventions that must be adhered to. Strangely, though she was determined not to admit it, she, too, felt a stirring of memory of him . . . but dismissed it out of hand. Where could she have met a man of his obvious standing!

'I am Ralph Densham, son and heir to this delightful abode, at your service!'

Before Katherine could respond, her arm was touched from behind and she turned to find Reverend Burrows at her side.

'Allow me to present our ward, Miss

Katherine Newcombe,' he said coolly.

Ralph made another bow, a sardonic gleam in his eyes.

Katherine sensed that a brief curtsey was in order and gracefully performed such, thankful for Reverend Burrows' support, though, at the same time, she wondered at the undercurrents between the two men. There was almost a bristling of tension between them.

'Come, Katherine. Sarah requests your presence in the ballroom,' George Burrows now murmured.

The two men bowed briefly again and George led Katherine through the ante-room to the ballroom, where the musicians were already striking up a lively tune.

Katherine watched the swaying figures on the floor, moving in a repeated pattern of movements. It looked so elegant and graceful! She found herself anticipating the next sequence of the dance and realised that, with practice, she would be able to make a creditable performance if she were asked to dance.

The next dance was *Sir Roger De Coverley*, a dance she had learned at school, and was delighted when a hesitant young man bowed in front of Sarah and asked if he might have the pleasure of leading her ward on to the floor.

From then on, the spaces in Katherine's card were swiftly being filled and, hoping that Mr Westcott had been invited to the ball, she was beginning to fear that if he didn't make an appearance soon, she would have no dances left to offer him.

At last she spotted him whilst performing a far-from-perfect performance in a quadrille and she smiled her acknowledgement of him. No sooner had she been taken back to Sarah's side than he was there before them.

He bowed to Sarah and enquired after her comfort and enjoyment of the evening so far, adding how much he had enjoyed beginning to build the raft with her three older children and hoped that they might be allowed to continue.

'Maybe Miss Newcombe might find the task enjoyable?' he continued, turning to include her in the conversation.

'Oh, yes! That would be delightful.' Katherine beamed, her eyes shining with the anticipation of a succession of such meetings. 'With not having any brothers, I have never had the opportunity to learn such skills.'

'Nor need you!' Sarah laughed, delicately waving her fan. 'I was surprised that Phoebe enjoyed it so!'

'We all have the urge to create, Mrs Burrows,' Mr Westcott assured her. 'Someone has created this beautiful ballroom and, no doubt, someone else has created a splendid feast through those doors over there, which brings me to my present hope of dancing the last dance before supper with Miss Newcombe and escorting her in to the aforesaid feast . . . unless, of course, it is already taken.' His glance was now entirely upon Katherine and her face was already showing disappointed regret.

Sarah had already bade Katherine to leave free the dance before supper and she had gladly complied, thinking Sarah probably wished to have her assistance at that time. She now looked from Mr Westcott to Sarah, half in plea, half in apology.

Sarah answered for her.

'I'm afraid I have made prior claim upon Miss Newcombe for that pleasure.' She smiled. 'However I'm sure she will be able to offer you a different dance.'

Katherine concealed her disappointment and opened her dance-card, glad to be able to show that she had been no wallflower as she waited for his appearance . . . a fact that he was swift to appreciate.

'I can see my tardy arrival has done me disservice!' He smiled. 'My only consolation is that I could have danced no more than two dances with you, anyway . . . and I claim them immediately. This third next one, here . . . and the second after supper.'

The longed-for time arrived and her expression of true pleasure was visible for all to see. The touch of his hand seemed to send a tingle of delight coursing through her whole body, bringing a pink blush to her cheeks, heightening the blue of her eyes.

They did not speak many words . . . there seemed no need. Their eyes spoke all that they wished to say. Never had Katherine felt so happy.

'I hope I am not too forward in asking this . . . but dare I hope that you think of me as Miles?' Mr Westcott asked a little hesitantly.

Katherine blushed prettily. She liked his unassuming nature and found him very easy to be with, even though she had little experience of conversation with men of his standing.

'I haven't dared!' she candidly admitted. 'But I would like to do so! Do you think of me as Katherine?'

Her voice was teasing a little and a faint tinge of colour on his face told her the answer before he spoke.

'I must admit that I do. I have done so since our first meeting!'

Katherine sighed happily and their smiling eyes showed each other their mutual attraction and delight.

Their dance ended far too soon, but the promise of their next one after supper made their temporary separation bearable.

Soon after the supper dance had started, Katherine was almost unnerved when she saw Ralph Densham approaching her and she swiftly stepped behind Sarah's chaise-longue, thankful to have a genuine excuse to refuse.

Undeterred by her manoeuvre, Ralph bowed before Sarah and requested her permission to lead Katherine on to the floor. Katherine was amazed to hear her agree, adding that it would be an honour indeed.

'You go, my dear! George will be able to take care of me, I am sure!'

Katherine felt a quiver of annoyance, wishing that Sarah had made the offer for Mr Westcott . . . but she had been too well-reared to commit the unforgivable social sin of refusing to stand up with a partner without proper excuse. She curtsied with quiet dignity but did not return Sarah's conspiratorial smile of encouragement.

'You dance delightfully, Miss Newcombe,' Ralph murmured in her ear, holding her far too close for decorum. 'I have been watching you, awaiting my turn patiently. Had you noticed? I saw your eyes searching the crowd . . . which is why I begged your patroness to have pity on me during your previous dance.'

His fingers tightened over her hand, seeming to impart some hidden signal or meaning.

Katherine cared for neither. She pulled her fingers free as they turned in opposite directions at the top of the set.

'You flatter yourself!' she said shortly, when they met again at the bottom of the set, not liking his proprietorial manner. 'I was searching for a . . . friend.'

His eyes hardened slightly.

'Indeed! May I ask whom? I understood you to be newly arrived here. Barely a week ago, wasn't it?'

'It was,' Katherine agreed, wondering from whom he had acquired the information and feeling no desire to give Miles' name to him.

His eyebrow rose at her brief reply, her lack of response not evading him. His lips smiled, though it did not reach his eyes. They parted company again, though Katherine was aware that his eyes followed her as she made her way down the outside of the set.

'I can see I will have to dance attendance on you more readily,' he murmured as they met once more. 'Is that the game you wish to play, my little flower?'

'I do not believe in playing games, sir!' she replied boldly.

'Neither do I,' he murmured softly. 'But, nonetheless, I shall pay you court, with your patron's permission, of course! You have an account to settle, methinks!'

Katherine glanced at him sharply, wondering what he meant but he merely smiled crookedly, his eyelids veiling his eyes.

Unlike the previous dance, this one seemed to go on for ever and the end of the music spelled no release for Katherine. Wishing she could slip away to Sarah's side, she was compelled to walk gracefully at his side as he led her from the floor and into second place behind his parents in the formal procession into the banqueting hall.

Katherine felt all eyes upon her and could sense the buzz of questions about her identity circulating around the room. Much as she wished to run from the room, she knew she must not shame Sarah and Reverend Burrows by such an ill-mannered act and she stayed quietly at Ralph's side, hardly able to nibble the many delicacies he placed upon her plate.

At one moment she saw Miles looking at her and her partner, his face puzzled. Katherine squirmed inside. He must think she had refused him the supper dance and had saved it for Ralph. Not wanting to draw Ralph's attention to him, she merely shook her head slightly, hoping he would recognise her distress at the situation in which she found herself. She saw his lips tighten and he turned away.

Her involuntary, 'Oh!' drew Ralph's attention and, before Katherine had the presence of mind to place her gaze elsewhere, Ralph followed the line of direction of her glance.

His eyes narrowed and his mouth set in a straight line but he made no comment.

Guests were beginning to drift back into the ballroom and Katherine murmured her excuses to Ralph, intending to find Sarah and to offer her assistance to anything she might require.

Ralph gripped her elbow firmly.

'Not so fast, my dear Katherine. The duration of the next dance is mine also.'

The familiar use of her christian

name, without him asking permission as Miles had done, increased Katherine's unease of him. She longed to be free of him and hastily spoke the first excuse she could think of.

'It is very hot in here, sir. I beg of you to excuse me and allow me to retire to the ladies' room for some moments.'

Ralph raised an enquiring eyebrow, as though reading her thoughts. His lips curled slightly. 'Through here,' he invited.

He pushed open a glass-panelled door and ushered Katherine through. They were in a long glass-domed room that, in daylight, would overlook the garden . . . though, at this time of year and evening, only the reflection of the room was to be seen in the wall of windows that ran the length of the room.

Exotic plants were growing in large tubs, arranged in groups, creating a meandering path from one end of the room to the other. Before Katherine had taken in how isolated the room was, Ralph had led her along a few twists of the path.

'But . . . where are we?' she asked, sensing that they ought not to be in such an unchaperoned situation. She made a move to return the way they had come but Ralph seized hold of her arm, restraining her movement.

'There's no need to run away. No-one will see us in here.'

His words only served to further alarm her and she faced him indignantly.

'I have no wish to remain here!'

Ralph laughed. 'There is nothing to fear. My parents and a few hundred others are within fifty feet of us!' He lowered his head slightly, tilting up her chin towards him. 'Those pretty eyes have beguiled me all evening . . . and your lips have been begging for a kiss!'

He drew her closer and before she fully realised his intent, he had covered her lips with his own.

Katherine went rigid with shock. She pulled away as soon as she was able.

'Sir! How dare you! You insult me!'

Ralph stood back and spread his hands, a look of amusement on his face.

'What is a kiss between friends? Your pretty smiles enticed me to think my attentions were desired. I only claimed what I thought you were willing to give.'

Katherine was confused. Had she somehow led him to think that? She hadn't done so deliberately. Neither was she aware of anything he might have misconstrued. But his light-hearted reaction robbed her of her anger, replacing it with confused regret. In her innocence, she must have implied a willingness to flirt with him. Even so, she backed away from him.

'No. No, I didn't mean to! You have misread me, sir!' Her cheeks flamed with heat. How embarrassing! 'Oh, dear! I must go!'

She turned and ran back the way they had come. Just as she reached out for the door, it opened inwards towards her and she had to step back, realising only then that Ralph had followed her flight and was standing behind her.

Framed in the doorway, their shocked expressions revealing their inner thoughts were Miles and a young lady whom Katherine didn't immediately recognise.

It was the young lady's outraged cry of, 'So, this is what you are doing, you hussy! I might have known it!' that brought her identity back to Katherine's memory. She was Eliza, the spoiled girl who had travelled with her on the coach from Honiton.

5

Miles spoke not a word. He took hold of Katherine's hand and drew her towards him.

'I have come to claim my dance,' he said evenly.

Katherine's mouth dropped open in surprise. Recalling her manners and social etiquette, she immediately closed it . . . but although the action composed her features, it didn't quieten her pounding heart. What must he think of her being closeted privately with a man? She knew her face must look fiery red with seeming guilt.

'Oh! N . . . no! I couldn't possibly dance with you now!' she demurred miserably.

Her free hand flew to cover the lower part of her face, her fingers spread over her lips and cheek. All she wanted to do was get away from the scene and recover her poise.

'Claiming your dance?' Eliza's voice cried out scornfully. 'She's nothing better than a trollop dressed up to ape her betters! A penniless servant, she said! Huh!'

Other people were gathering near, drawn to the scene by Eliza's strident tones. All eyes were upon them, their shocked faces matching her own feelings. She didn't yet know any of their faces . . . but they would all know who she was! She was bringing disgrace upon Reverend Burrows and Sarah!

Miles' lips tightened.

'You speak out of turn, madam!' he said coldly, trying once more to draw Katherine away . . . but her feet felt rooted to the floor and her legs immobile. It felt like a scene from a nightmare!

Eliza's face took on a triumphant expression.

'I know what it is! I was right after all! You were in league with the highwayman who robbed us! That is why you are attired thus!'

'No!'

Katherine's small gasp of denial was overshadowed by a louder exclamation behind her.

'Don't talk ridiculously, woman!' Ralph Densham snapped. 'Such malicious talk is dangerous . . . and founded on nothing more than spite, I warrant!'

He turned his back on Eliza, once more facing Katherine. He made a curt bow.

'Your servant, Miss Newcombe!' His face softened slightly and he added softly, 'We will speak further on the matter . . . at a more propitious time.' Bowing stiffly to the assembled crowd, he strode away purposefully.

Katherine was hardly aware of his parting sentence. Her face was now white, her eyes wide with shock at the escalation of the incident.

'I must go!' she said desperately, her head down.

She remembered little of her flight. Somewhere on the edge of the assembled crowd she saw Reverend Burrows, a mildly curious expression on his face as he drew nearer.

'Please! Take me to Sarah!' she begged.

'What has been happening over there?' he asked curiously.

'N . . . nothing! A small contretemps! I will tell you later!'

She couldn't even try to explain there and then. She would burst into tears and, having so far managed to hold them at bay, she didn't want further indignity to cloud her evening.

'Sarah has been carried to the ladies' rest room,' Reverend Burrows told her. 'I will show you the way.'

Katherine was grateful that he didn't press for an answer and also thankful to gain the sanctuary of the rest room. She found Sarah being attended to by two matronly women who were fussing over her, rearranging her skirt and plumping up the pillows behind her. She looked tired and admitted so to Katherine.

'I am sorry to bring your evening to a close, dear . . . but I have suddenly found the excitement too much for me.' She smiled faintly, spreading her hands helplessly.

Her own problem pushed aside, Katherine took hold of Sarah's hand and seated herself carefully on the edge of the chaise-longue.

'I don't mind in the slightest. I can see how tired you look. Are you glad you came?'

Sarah smiled. 'Yes, indeed! It gave me so much pleasure to see you dancing and looking so pretty!'

Katherine could think of no reply that wouldn't need explaining, so she wisely refrained from answering. She merely smiled modestly, knowing that she must explain all that had happened as soon as possible . . . before embellished accounts began to fly around the village!

★   ★   ★

It was after midnight when Katherine at last sank into her bed and was able to think about all that had happened. Her earlier happiness had been marred by the unpleasantness of the final hour. With no-one to witness her sorrow, she allowed her tears to fall unheeded.

All the dreams she had dared to hope would come true were now in shatters. Neither Miles nor anyone else would wish to be associated with her in future!

Daylight brought hope, but it was Sunday. There was no question of failing to attend the morning service in the village church.

Getting the children washed, dressed and breakfasted was no mean task. They plied her with unceasing questions about the previous evening's entertainment.

She had thought about having to face many who had been at the ball and had decided that a dignified silence would be her best option. Whatever she had done wrong, it had been unintentional and she would let Sarah and Reverend

Burrows be the ones to settle her fate.

But that was impossible until after lunch. Katherine would have to hope that anyone with anything to say would leave it until another occasion.

Dressed in her new walking-out outfit, Katherine followed behind the wheelchair, holding Phoebe's and Grace's hands and ushering forwards Henry and Zachary.

They behaved throughout the service and, throughout the sermon, the only sounds coming from their pew was the squeak of stylus upon slate as the older three drew a picture and Grace played with her doll.

It was thoughts of after the service that held captive Katherine's imagination. If it were anything like her church at home, only the most inclement weather would prevent people from gathering outside to spend time in friendly gossip.

Katherine wondered if it was her imagination that people were glancing her way and looking away again quickly, their heads nodding as they exchanged comments about her. She felt extremely uncomfortable.

'Shall I wheel you home, Sarah?' Katherine asked at length, not wanting anyone to say anything to Sarah about the previous evening's debacle before she had had the chance to tell her herself.

Sarah turned to glance over her shoulder.

'Oh, that's a good idea, Katherine. Thank you, dear.'

'Good morning, ladies!'

It was Miles, raising his hat to them. Katherine had seen him in a pew towards the back of the church but had cast down her eyes as she passed him, not wanting to see the tight-lipped look of disapproval that had been evident on his face the previous evening.

Her breath now caught in her throat as she wondered if he was going to express his disapproval of her to Sarah. His attention was on Sarah, not herself, but her fears were proved unfounded when he continued, 'I would count it a pleasure to wheel your chair to the vicarage. May I?'

'Why, certainly, Mr Westcott! And it gives me the opportunity to thank you again for the attention you have given our children. They haven't yet stopped talking about the raft-building!'

Miles laughed. 'Thank you! I'm sure they will resume to normal when they have to recite their seven-times table tomorrow morning! But the pleasure was mine. As I said last evening, I hope I have your permission to continue next Saturday, weather permitting, of course?'

'You have! Though I'm not sure George will be able to accompany the children every Saturday.'

Miles had already taken hold of the handles of the wheelchair and had begun to push it up the gentle slope. Katherine hung back, her hands outstretched towards Phoebe and Grace, glad to have the excuse to follow more slowly, not wanting to put Miles . . . Mr Westcott, she had better resume to call him . . . into the uncomfortable position of being forced to be pleasant to her.

She could hear Miles and Sarah chatting pleasantly and was miserably wishing she could put back the clock to this time yesterday and refuse to go to the ball . . . when she became aware that Miles had partly turned the wheel-chair around and that both he and Sarah were looking at her expectantly.

'P . . . pardon?' she stammered. 'I'm sorry. Did you address me?' She looked from one to the other.

Which one had asked the question? And what was it? Was it something about last night?

Sarah chuckled at her dilemma.

'Mr Westcott asked my permission to allow him to invite you for a stroll along the riverside this afternoon. I said that he may . . . as long as you take Phoebe and Grace, since I cannot chaperone you. Don't worry! I won't inflict Henry and Zachary on you!'

Katherine felt her cheek redden. 'Oh! Y . . . yes. Yes, of course!'

91

★ ★ ★

As soon as lunch was over, Katherine asked if she might speak to Sarah and Reverend Burrows. She wanted to clear the issue from her conscience and was willing to be admonished if necessary.

Although Sarah was puzzled by Katherine's request, Reverend Burrows seemed less so.

'I don't know why Ralph Densham behaved as he did,' she stated honestly. 'He said he thought me to have sought him out and flirted with him . . . though in all conscience, I had no such intention. As for Eliza's accusation that I was in league with the highwayman, it is quite nonsensical but I will abide by your decision as to what is to become of me.'

Sarah seemed utterly surprised at her admission. Reverend Burrows nodded his head.

'Some parishioners did murmur their disquiet this morning,' he agreed. 'I told them that they had completely misinterpreted the incident and that the other young lady had clearly mistaken you for someone else. There will be no further reference to it, have no fear.'

Katherine's relief was evident.

'Was I at fault, do you think?'

'Only in your innocence and trusting nature,' Reverend Burrows assured her. 'I must admit I feared you might attract Ralph's attentions . . . and I don't think his interest in you has ended yet.'

Sarah looked at her husband in astonishment.

Sarah agreed. She smiled teasingly. 'I think Mr Westcott thinks highly of you. You may do better there!'

Katherine blushed.

It was two o'clock when Mr Westcott presented himself at the front door of the vicarage. Katherine had the two girls ready for an afternoon walk and Sarah bade them be on their way in order to make best use of the light.

The two girls skipped ahead, knowing the way down to the river. Katherine was glad of Mr Westcott's arm as she carefully descended down the stony track. It wasn't unduly steep but, with the recent rain, it was wet and slippery.

Miles' manner was cordial and her anxiety about his reason for wishing to walk with her was fading fast.

'You called me Miles last night,' he reproved her when she used his formal title.

'That was before . . . you know . . . what happened!'

'And you think it makes a difference?'

Katherine looked away. 'You seemed very disapproving of me!'

'Not of you, you dear girl! Though I certainly disapprove of the other young lady! Whatever was she referring to?'

Katherine explained about the hold-up on the Honiton to Sidmouth coach and Eliza's accusation at the time, mainly because Katherine had shown little fear and had been fortunate enough to have nothing worth stealing.

'Then half the population of England

must be in league with him!' Miles declared.

'Or half of Ottersleigh!' Katherine pointed out. 'Has it occurred to you that this village is far wealthier than the average village?'

Miles shook his head.

'I haven't thought about it, but everyone has been very generous with me, helping me to settle in. I put it down to their Christian charity.'

'Maybe that's all it is,' Katherine agreed, not wanting any disagreement to spoil their afternoon. 'Everyone is certainly very kind.'

The stony path continued along the riverbank. There was room for two people to walk side by side and Katherine was very conscious of her hand resting gently on Miles' crooked arm.

The river was flowing strongly in the same direction as they were walking.

'It's the ebb tide,' Miles explained. 'It's a tidal river, flowing down from off the moors, but is also fed from the sea.

You should see it in a storm! I've heard that the bridge just ahead there has been washed away more than once when a storm has coincided with a full tide! I've been reading some historical notes about the village and river, intending to teach the children their own local history, as well as our national history.

'Do you know, as recently as up to 1778, the river was navigable for a few miles inland and it was only after the river had silted up that the present lower bridge was constructed. You will find shipwrights and caulkers listed among other local tradesmen in the church registers of births and deaths.'

He looked down at her eagerly-listening face and decided to tease her with further information. 'It has also been hinted that there was a thriving trade in smuggled goods as far inland as Colaton Raleigh. That's where Sir Walter Raleigh of Elizabethan times was born and spent his childhood. It's just a mile or so up river.'

'Smugglers? Really? Your boys will love to learn about that! What a pity you didn't teach when Ben Gillard was at school! It would have given him a third choice of career!' She laughingly explained about Ben's desire to be either a highwayman or a pirate, whichever opportunity presented itself first.

Miles laughed with her.

'I'd better be careful then, or I shall have a horde of angry parents on my back, blaming me for being a bad influence on their sons.'

Miles lifted Grace up on to his shoulders and Katherine held Phoebe's hand. It had been a lovely afternoon walk and Katherine knew she would close her eyes that night with Miles' face imprinted on her memory.

★　★　★

It was pitch dark when Katherine felt herself to be suddenly wide awake. She had been dreaming of smugglers, no doubt because of Miles' discourse about them, and, as part of her dream, she heard muted footfalls upon the gravel path that ran around the vicarage. It took a moment or two before she realised that she was now awake . . . and the noises were still there.

Unable to restrain herself, she left her bed and padded over to the window. Her breath caught in her throat. There were people out there! Shadowy figures flitted out of the cover of the trees and were lost from view as they went round the side of the house.

Reaching out for her cloak, Katherine slipped it around her shoulders and hurried to the door of her room. If she reached the front landing window quickly enough, she might see them emerge at the front of the house.

She hurried silently along the landing to the head of the stairs, intending to go down to the mid-level to peer out of the small windowpanes. Instead, she ran straight into the soft body of a man!

'Oh!'

'What is the matter, Katherine?'

To her relief, it was Reverend Burrows' voice. Katherine's thudding heart began to settle. Had he heard the noises, too, and had come to investigate?

'There are people out there! Men! What are they doing? Come and see!'

She made as if to go down the stairs but Reverend Burrows put his hand on her shoulder to prevent her.

'There is no-one there, Katherine. Go back to bed!'

'But I saw them!'

'It's a trick of the wind blowing the evergreen bushes. No-one is there. I have looked.'

Katherine turned back to her room. She looked again through her bedroom window but all was still and dark.

It was only when Katherine was tucked up once more under her blankets that the thought came to her that Reverend Burrows had been dressed in his outdoor clothes . . .

And, when she referred to the incident the following day, Reverend Burrows denied all knowledge of the occurrence whatsoever.

'You must have been dreaming, Katherine . . . after hearing the tales our young Mr Westcott was telling you!'

Katherine was puzzled. Was that what it was? A dream?

6

Henry and Zachary had seized upon Katherine's retelling of Miles' talk about smugglers on her return the previous afternoon and, their imaginations fired, they were eager to hear more. By the time they came home for their lunch, Mr Westcott had agreed to research the local historical records and use his contacts in the educational world to discover any other true stories about smuggling.

By Wednesday evening, a number of parents had complained to the school board about Mr Westcott over-glamorising the trade and inciting their sons, and a few daughters, to make it their, albeit temporary, life's ambition to be smugglers.

Reverend Burrows didn't quote their exact words, but he strongly advised Miles to change to a different topic

. . . something less controversial.

Reluctantly, Miles agreed, but he grumbled about it to Katherine the next day when she lingered at the school gate after sending the children up the lane to the vicarage.

'They said they would be happier to have their children learning about the Civil War, as they had done! As if that weren't twice as bloodthirsty!'

Henry and Zachary weren't dissuaded quite so easily and, on Saturday afternoon, when they were once more down by the river helping to bind some of the logs together, they plied their teacher with constant questions about why, how, when and where the smugglers of old smuggled their goods.

If the skull and crossbones they designed for the raft's flag was anything to go by, it was clear that smuggling and piracy were closely associated in their thinking.

Ben Gillard had joined them by this time and he added the lore of highwayman to the discussion and his standing with the two younger boys rose immediately. He promised to return next week to help some more and Katherine wished again that he had had someone to fire his interest more when he had been attending school.

Miles had found his own interest quickened by the local aspect of the subject and on the first wet Saturday, when the raft-building had to be suspended, he took the coach to Exeter with the intentions of researching the local news-sheets for further information.

He imparted his findings to Katherine when they met briefly before and after school and in more detail on the following Saturday, along with an item of news of personal interest to her.

'I read in last week's news-sheet that the highwayman who had been terrorising these parts recently . . . you know, the one who held up your coach . . . was winged by a well-aimed shot from the coach-driver on the Exeter to Honiton route.'

Katherine was surprised to see Ben's reaction to the news. He looked anxious . . . or fearful. Did he idolise the man for his daring audacity? Then the look passed and she turned her attention back to Miles.

'Was he captured?'

'No. He managed to ride away but no doubt it will stop his activities for a while.

'And, apparently, there is a sailor called Sam Mutter who is local to Sidmouth and is on many a wanted list for his smuggling activities,' Miles continued to pass on information he had discovered. 'He seems to come and go as he pleases. The authorities suspect that he has more than one way of getting his illegal goods ashore, since the traps laid at Sidmouth have failed to apprehend him. One idea is that he has a hideaway up on the heathland.'

'Where's that?'

'Not far away from here apparently. A mile or so farther up the road out of the village past the vicarage, the article said.

Passaford Lane, just past Pavey's Farm, leads up to it through a plantation of trees.'

The look in Miles' eyes warmed Katherine's heart. She knew she was falling in love with him and, although such things had not yet been spoken between them, she felt that he, too, was not averse to her.

He behaved very circumspectly but his hand lingered on hers at times and she didn't discourage him. When he turned to offer her his hand as they descended to the river, Katherine smiled to herself. She didn't really need his assistance but it was very nice to feel the strength of his arm around her waist or the support of his arm under her hand.

She was already looking forward to the Christmas ball with eager anticipation. She would be better prepared this time to avert any unacceptable advances. Not that she expected Ralph Densham to still have any interest in her. She had heard that he had been away somewhere . . . and hopefully, he would stay away, she thought uncharitably.

'Can we look for smugglers?' Henry demanded.

Katherine looked at him in surprise, her thoughts having transported her far away to balls and dancing and pretty gowns. 'Pardon?'

'Up to the moor, when you go looking for the smugglers!'

Katherine laughed.

'We'll leave that to the authorities! But, yes, you can come with us if and when we go up there . . . if your parents approve.' She knew that it wouldn't be considered seemly for her to be accompanied on such an expedition by Miles alone.

'You don't want to be going up there,' Ben warned. 'There's old lime pits and bogs to fall into. Folk get lost and are never seen again, especially if the mist comes down.'

The weather seemed determined to worsen rather than improve. They were now well into December and the wind and rain combined to keep the children indoors both in and out of school hours, curtailing any activity on the river.

The raft was completed and had made its maiden voyage across the river. Jacob Gillard, Ben's father, and Nick Conybear, the miller, had been pressed into service and had slung a long rope securely across the river from the upper branches of two stout oak trees at a wide point where the current ran more slowly.

The rope could be lowered to adult height only, so that the raft could be manoeuvred across the river by pulling on the rope, hand over hand. Another strong rope was fastened to the rear of the raft and secured to around the trunk of another stout tree. This rope limited the length of journey the raft could make and enabled it to be drawn back to its mooring place.

All the children of the village had enjoyed its launching and had received suitable instructions regarding its use . . . the main one being that the raft had never to be used without at least one adult being present and, to date, no-one had violated the rule.

The second Tuesday night in December saw more heavy rainfall and after taking the children to school, Katherine walked down into the village with the intent of purchasing some off-cuts of cloth to make into handkerchiefs for gifts to give out at Christmas. She had already embroidered some pieces of light cotton for all female recipients and fashioned a tiny edging of lace around the edges.

Now, she needed some plainer stuff to edge simply with neat stitches for Miles and Reverend Burrows. She had made small bags of toffee for Henry and Zachary, correctly anticipating that a hand-stitched handkerchief would seem dull stuff to the two lively boys.

As she crossed the river over the stone bridge next to the huge watermill, she noticed how high the river was running. A number of fallen branches had been swept into the river and these were causing a jamming effect under the bridge, making an even larger amount of build-up of more flotsam on the upstream side of the bridge. This in turn was causing the river to break its banks, the water spreading out over the river path and backing upstream towards where the vicarage, church and school stood.

Katherine knew that the buildings were set far enough back from the river bank to be out of immediate danger but she thought of where the raft was moored. If it were dislodged from its mooring and swept into the river, it would cause even more jamming and, in addition, the hard work of the children would be wasted.

The rain had temporarily ceased to fall and without any more ado, her purchases forgotten, she set off along the riverside to see if she could avert new disaster.

She could see the mooring position of the raft up ahead. The river was much wider there than usual and the raft, instead of being safely grounded, as they had left it after its most recent use, was already bobbing about, still secured to its mooring but being slowly pulled by the fast-moving current into the main stream.

She wasn't sure what made her look beyond the raft to where a wooden bridge spanned the river about one hundred yards farther upstream. Maybe the sound of something attracted her attention, though she wasn't aware of it at the time. As she looked, however, the wooden bridge seemed to take on a life of its own.

It rose in the middle, breaking and splintering as it did so. Its supporting under-structure buckled and broke; the walkway, wooden planks nailed to the frame, fractured and ripped apart.

Amidst the wreckage now tumbling towards her was the floundering body of a man. The wreckage of the bridge added to the turbulence of the water and even if the man had been able to swim, the confines of his position made it impossible. He was swept along helplessly, his arms sometimes flailing at the air and then submerged under the torrent.

Without making a conscious decision to attempt a rescue, she picked up the hem of her skirt and ran forward towards the raft.

The overhead rope was hanging loosely, already dislodged, but still attached to the trees on the opposite side of the river. Unheeding of her own safety, she waded into the water and scrambled on to the raft, unaware of tearing her skirt and scraping the skin off her hands.

Unlike when the raft had been jubilantly launched on to the water, it now dipped and swirled, but she managed to stand upright and grab hold of the overhead rope as the raft spun underneath it. The rope burned her hands and wrenched at her wrists but she held on.

The man was very close now.

It was no use calling out to him to try

to grasp hold of the raft as he passed. He wouldn't have heard and, in the time available, he wouldn't have understood.

Katherine knew that the minute she let go of the rope, the current would pull the raft into its headlong tumbling rush and she would have no control on its direction. She had to time letting go with the man being within arm's reach of her . . . and there would be no second chance. And, if she were pulled into the river, she knew she would drown . . . both her and the man she was hoping to rescue.

She steadied her feet, tensed her arms . . . and let go, falling forwards on to her stomach, her arms out-stretched. It happened too quickly to be sure of anything, but she could feel the softness of cloth in her hands and she gripped hold of it tightly, hoping that if she were indeed holding the man's jacket, that it was fastened securely around him.

She felt the raft jerk under her as it reached the end of the length of mooring rope. The jerk swung the raft

112

around towards the bank, easing the strain of the pull of the man's weight upon her arms.

'Grab hold!' she yelled at the man. 'Grab hold! Quickly! I've got you!'

Her voice must have penetrated into his mind for he made clumsy movements with his arms and managed to get them over the raised edge of the raft. Katherine hauled him under his armpits. He was a dead weight. The raft swung some more, into shallower water, enabling the man to heave himself farther on board, where he collapsed on to his knees and flopped forwards.

At the same moment, the rope holding the raft gave way and the raft spun with the current into the fast-raging torrent, tipping and rising uncontrollably on the turbulent mass.

They were being swept down towards the bridge. If they could get lodged behind the debris that was already lodged there, Katherine hoped they might have time to jump ashore.

There was a man on the bridge . . . Nick

Conybear, the miller, Katherine thought. She stood up and waved her arms above her head.

'Help us!' she cried.

She doubted the man heard . . . but she saw him run off the bridge, down the bank and struggle into the river where the branches were jammed together. The raft thudded into the mass, momentarily halting its progress.

It wouldn't hold for long. There was a sound of grating and tearing and in front of her eyes, Katherine saw the stone bridge beginning to break up and tumble into the swell.

'Jump!' Nick Conybear shouted to her.

'Grab him!' Katherine yelled.

The man was on his knees, head towards the miller.

Nick reached out and grabbed hold of the man under his left armpit. Katherine held him around his right upper arm. She leaped . . . staggered . . . and fell.

The three of them were in the water.

Katherine felt herself sinking, weighed down by the weight of her skirt and cloak. She was in a circling eddy, not quite in the main current and a number of broken branches and other wreckage were jammed together, with her in the midst. Some instinct for survival made her heave herself higher on to the jammed logs.

'Hold on!' Nick shouted above the roar of the water. 'The bridge is going!'

7

With an added roar and a crash, the main structure of the road bridge collapsed into the river, sending a wave of water back upstream. It was that wave of water that threw the three of them farther up the bank.

Katherine felt every bone in her body jar as she fell upon tree trunks and boulders that had been washed downstream with the raging torrent. She lay winded, unable to even think of moving.

'Thank you, missy! I'll not forget thee!'

Katherine had no breath to reply. Someone, she knew not who, picked her up and slung her uncomfortably over his shoulder and struggled up the high bank with her. Someone else assisted the stranger and Nick Conybear up to the road. The bridge was completely gone; Nick's mill, that stood on the river bank, now teetered on the edge; the mill leat was gone; the wooden water-wheel was gone.

Someone, Ben it turned out, had run to The Blue Anchor and come back with the small dray. The stranger, Nick and Katherine were assisted aboard and swiftly transported to the inn, where warm blankets were wrapped around them and they were hustled into its warm interior.

Since Katherine was the only woman in need of warmth and rest, Mrs Gillard took her into their private parlour, where she stripped her of her clothes, briskly rubbed her dry and seated her in a cosy armchair by the fire wrapped in more warm blankets.

'Eh, your poor hands, dearie!' Mrs Gillard gasped. 'Ye'll not be doing much with them for a while! Wait here while I get something to put on them.'

The soothing cream that Mrs Gillard smoothed gently on to the palms of her hands eased the pain a little. Katherine felt helpless as her hands were then swathed in bandages. She would be no use to anybody for quite a while.

A small pewter mug of something that almost lifted the roof of her mouth off was held at her lips. Whatever it was, Katherine could feel its fiery warmth spreading down her throat to her stomach and outwards to all parts of her body.

She felt utterly tired and, though meaning to close her eyes for only a minute, she fell fast asleep. Her last conscious thought was that she hoped the man she had rescued was making a good recovery and that he would be none the worse for his misadventure.

It was dark when Katherine awoke.

The fire was burning brightly, casting shadows on the wall. For a few moments, Katherine couldn't think where she was. Then, it all came back. Strangely, she now felt more frightened by the experience than she had while it was happening.

The door opened and Mrs Gillard

popped her head around.

'There you are, dearie! Wide awake at last, are you? And here's a young man come to see you! I'll leave the door ajar so that no improprieties can be talked about, but don't 'ee worry none. I'll see that nobody comes near!'

With that, she withdrew her head and Katherine was thankful to see Miles framed in the doorway.

'Oh, Miles! I'm so glad to see you!' she cried, and, to her utter embarrassment, she burst into tears.

Miles strode across the room and gathered her into his arms.

'My love! My darling! My brave girl! Hush, now! Don't cry!'

He stroked her hair and buried his face into it, not even noticing that it was stiff with silted river water and lacking its usually fragrant scent.

Katherine clung to him with her bandaged hands, not caring that it might be considered too forward of her! She needed the comfort of his arms around her and the manly strength of his body supporting her. When she lifted up her face to look at him she felt overwhelmed by the tenderness of love in his eyes and felt herself almost drowning in the depth of his eyes.

In spite of that, she was surprised but not displeased, when he gently laid his lips upon her and tenderly kissed her. Such a wonderful feeling spiralled around her body. Her bones felt as though they were melting. Oh, the terror of it all was worth it if this was to be the reward!

'You could have died! I could have lost you!' Miles murmured against her as he nuzzled his lips against her cheek and down the curve of her neck.

'I know, I know. It was quite dreadful! I was trapped among the wreckage and couldn't get out . . . and then, it was like an unseen hand picking me up and flinging me and the other two on to the river bank!'

Her breath caught in her throat at the memory . . . and then another thought flashed into her mind.

'Oh, and just think . . . if I hadn't gone to check on the raft, that poor man would have probably drowned! He would have been completely swept away. How is he? Is he quite recovered?'

Miles drew away from her slightly, a puzzled expression on his face.

'Man? What man? Nick Conybear, do you mean? He's all right.'

'No, not Nick! The man who was swept into the river! The wooden bridge, just upstream from where the raft was moored, was swept away just as I neared there. The man fell with it into the swollen river. That's why I got on to the raft! I knew it was the only way to give him a chance of rescue!'

Miles shook his head, his eyebrows furrowed.

'No-one has made mention of any other man! They said you had fallen into the river and got caught up in the debris by the bridge.' He looked at her doubtfully. 'I think maybe the shock of being in the water, and maybe a bang on your head.'

'I didn't bang my head!' she retorted indignantly. 'I may be suffering from shock! I don't doubt it! But I am not hallucinating! A man fell into the river and I pushed out the raft to save him! Ask Nick Conybear! He helped me to get him out of the river. And Ben . . . he brought the dray to bring us to the inn. Mrs Gillard saw him! She'll tell you!'

Katherine could hear her voice rising and felt quite hysterical at Miles' reaction to her protests. Why was he looking at her so pityingly?

He stroked her cheek and then held her chin between his thumb and forefinger, letting his lips gently brush over hers.

'I'll get Mrs Gillard back to you,' he said softly. 'A warm drink may help your mind to rest and recover.'

'I don't need . . . '

'Hush, darling. Don't worry!'

He tucked the blankets around her again and tip-toed to the door, as if he were leaving someone in their sickbed, Katherine decided in annoyance. Just let him wait until someone assured him that she was not rambling in delirium!

Mrs Gillard bustled into the room.

'There, now!' she said soothingly. 'We'll soon have thee all right, dearie. We're sending for the carriage from the manor house to take thee back to the vicarage. You'll be better there in familiar surroundings. A good night's rest will do no end of good, you see if it don't!'

'But, Mrs Gillard! What about the man?'

Katherine was sure they were keeping something from her. Maybe he had died and they didn't want to upset her.

She reached out her hand and said to Mrs Gillard, 'Please tell me! I won't be upset.'

Mrs Gillard shook her head regretfully.

'Don't ye worry your head none, Miss Newcombe. There was no man. No-one has died. We've been very lucky, what with the road bridge being swept away like that. As it is, the village is cut in two until the river goes down and we can get a make-shift bridge put across. At least you're on the right side of the river. We'll have thee home in no time!'

'But, Mrs Gillard, Nick Conybear! He was there! He helped to pull the man out! Let me speak with him.'

'Nick pulled you out of the water, m'dear. He saved your life! He'll have a few free drinks in here when word gets around, you mark my words!'

'But, Mrs Gillard, it wasn't like that! A man . . . '

But Mrs Gillard was on her way out of the room again.

'You just rest yourself for now, Miss Newcombe. You'll see it all straight in the morning with a good night's sleep behind you. You'll see!'

Katherine sank back against the cushions, her mind bewildered. There had been a man! There had! She could still see his face. It was round and swarthy. An outdoor man . . . possibly a seaman of some sort.

* * *

Lord Densham's coach arrived just after seven o'clock. A stocky woman of middle years bustled into the parlour followed by a younger woman who was carrying a bundle.

'Put it down on the table, Dorcas, and help Miss Newcombe out of those blankets. Now, let's get you dressed.'

'Those aren't my clothes,' Katherine protested weakly, feeling that everything was beyond her control. 'I'm sure my own will be dry by now.'

'Ruined they are, by all accounts, Miss Newcombe,' the older woman replied. 'These will do for now, Lady Densham will sort out what you're to wear tomorrow.'

'Lady Densham? Why should Lady Densham . . . ?'

'It's been decided that you are to come to Densham Manor for a few days until you recover, miss. You won't be much use to Mrs Burrows with hands like those. We'll take no chances, shall we? Come on, Dorcas, sharpen your wits! Hold the skirts so that Miss Newcombe can step into it!'

Finally she was clothed and Miles was allowed back into the parlour to carry her out to the carriage.

Feeling a little upset by his failure to believe her version of events, Katherine was cool towards him, though at any other time she would have savoured the experience of being carried in his arms to the full!

'I'll come to see you tomorrow after school, shall I?' he asked after he had deposited her on to the velvet-lined carriage seats.

His expression was anxious and Katherine relented slightly.

'I'm to stay at the manor for a few days,' she informed him, feeling incredulous that it was so. Her, a country parson's daughter to stay in the manor house!

'I'll still call, to make sure you're all right.'

He touched the side of her face gently and looked at her so tenderly that Katherine softened towards him.

'All right! Will you visit the vicarage and make sure Sarah can manage?'

'Of course!'

'Arrangements have been made for Mrs Burrows,' Mrs Besley said briskly. 'The second parlour maid has been sent down. Now, if you've quite finished, we'll be off! Fold up the step, young man, and close the door.'

When he had done so, she pulled a tasselled cord at the side of the door and the carriage jerked into movement.

They were at the manor house in no time at all, it seemed, and Katherine was once more lifted into a strong pair of arms and carried in through the kitchen door.

The kitchen and other downstairs rooms were a hive of activity. Katherine was relieved that they didn't pause and that she wasn't expected to speak to anyone. It suddenly seemed to be all too much and all she wanted was to be able to go to sleep. She was carried upstairs and deposited in a room slightly grander than her room at the vicarage.

Mrs Besley and Dorcas appeared again and helped her out of the outdoor clothes and into a lace-edged cotton nightdress.

'I'll be on the truckle-bed by the window if you need me later,' she heard Dorcas say . . . but in two seconds, she was fast asleep.

The morning had long broken when she next awoke. Dorcas was seated on a chair doing some mending but she put it down as soon as she realised that Katherine was awake.

'Good morning, miss!' she said brightly, stepping to the window and drawing back the curtains. 'And it's a brighter one today!'

After a bowl of porridge, followed by fingers of toast spread with butter and marmalade, Katherine was dressed in yet more borrowed clothing and was then led downstairs to Lady Densham's parlour, where Lady Densham greeted her warmly.

'Come and sit down by the fire, Miss Newcombe. We want you to feel quite at home whilst you are here,' she said kindly.

'You're being very kind, Lady Densham. Everyone is!' Katherine said to her. 'I feel that I'm putting everyone to a great deal of trouble.'

'Nonsense, my dear. We all help each other in this village. Maybe you'd like to tell me what you remember of what happened yesterday.'

Katherine was glad of the opportunity to repeat her version of the event, but was once again disappointed by its reception, when Lady Densham reached over and patted her hand.

'Now, don't be upset that your memory is still playing you false, dear. Sometimes our minds play tricks on us, especially when something like this happens. I am assured that no other man was involved in the incident, apart from Nick Conybear, who, thankfully, pulled you out of the river. A blow to the head can cause all sorts of delusions for a while!'

'But, I didn't have a blow to my head!' Katherine protested.

'I think that a glance in my hand-mirror will dispel that illusion, dear! Here, take a peep!'

Katherine took the ivory-backed mirror out of Lady Densham's hand and looked into it at her reflection. Her eyes widened with shock.

A stranger stared back at her . . . a stranger with a bruised, puffy face.

8

Miles made his way home feeling disgruntled and worried. Katherine had shown herself to be level-headed and reliable . . . but her word was now at variance with everybody else's who had been at the scene.

He hadn't had the heart to tell her that her bruised face showed that she had indeed been banged about her head . . . more than once! The question was, did that make her memory of the incident to be at fault? The problem was, if Katherine's version were correct, why did everybody else assert a different scenario? And where was the man whom Katherine had taken such a risk to save?

It was too dark to do any investigating now, but, if the weather improved, he would go down to the river first thing in the morning!

The following morning, Miles stood high on the riverbank. The river was still swollen with excess water and had burst its banks in numerous places. However, a few feet below where Miles was standing, the raft was still moored to a tree. It looked as though it had been butted and battered by passing debris but it was still intact.

Miles didn't know what he had expected to see. The absence of the raft wouldn't have proved Katherine's version, but its presence disproved it! He stroked his chin sadly. Katherine wouldn't like it!

It was decided that Katherine would stay at the manor until the day after the Christmas Ball, which was to be two days before Christmas.

Miles made the journey on foot whenever the weather allowed him to do so, though this wasn't as often as he would have liked. Chaperoned correctly as they were, by either Lady Densham herself or one of her more senior maids, the conversation between Miles and

Katherine was stilted and far from satisfactory.

Katherine had no wish to be ungrateful to Lord and Lady Densham, but she frequently wished herself to be back home at the vicarage. Her bruised body and face were slowly healing, having undergone changes of colour of every hue. Her hands were mending, albeit much more slowly, and still needed to be kept covered, which meant that she wasn't allowed to do anything other than walk in the garden if the weather was fine, or in the conservatory if it were not.

She was very much bored with this life of inactivity!

Whether this was the reason that she was snappy with Miles the last day but one before the ball, or whether it was because he made reference to the fact that the raft was still attached to its mooring, Katherine didn't know. She regretted her peevishness after he had taken his leave of her and perversely wished he were back at her side so that she might apologise profusely to him.

How could she blame him for believing what his eyes could see . . . when the only alternative was to listen to the ramblings of a confused young lady?

Her memory adhered to her initial tale and her mind replayed, time after time, the horrific sight of the wooden bridge surging upwards, with the sound of the splintering of wood as it broke into pieces, catapulting the luckless man into the churning waters.

Had she heard the sound in reality? Or was that her mind supplying the sound she expected to hear? And, if that were part of her imagination, was the remainder imagined also? Had she actually screamed as she remembered? Or was that also a trick of the mind? And the sight of the man tumbling down?

She had no problems with the rest of the drama. She could now remember falling into the river, albeit off the raft, not from the bank, and she could remember sinking down under the surface and coming up among the flotsam and jetsam of the storm . . . and, yes, she had banged her head on the logs. She had the bruises to prove it. So, why couldn't she accept that she was mistaken about the initial moments of the accident?

The evening before the ball, Lady Densham invited Katherine to join them in the dining-room for dinner.

'Your hands are nearly healed and need only to be covered in your fine cotton gloves . . . and you have for so long been excluded from Society that the numbers present at the ball tomorrow could overwhelm you, dear,' Lady Densham persuaded her. 'And it is only family, dear. There will be no need to stand upon ceremony. Dorcas will bring you a selection of gowns to try on. What a blessing that you and I are of similar build.'

For a woman more than twice her age, Lady Densham had very modern tastes of fashion, Katherine had noted, and plenty of gowns to choose from. She hadn't been presented with the same gown twice!

Partway through fastening the long row of buttons down the back of Katherine's gown — a pale turquoise concoction that fell in silky folds over her hips to her ankles, with a low décolleté that ended in tiny puff sleeves on both shoulders — Dorcas was called away by a whispered message from a downstairs maid.

'I won't be long, miss,' Dorcas apologised. 'Lady Densham has mislaid her fan and wants me to find it immediately.'

Katherine waited for her return but when she heard the dinner gong resounding from downstairs, she realised that she had been forgotten.

Not one to be fazed by a few unfastened buttons, Katherine decided she had better make her way downstairs and get someone down there to complete the fastenings.

A quick peep in the mirror showed

her to be more than presentable, especially with the borrowed necklace of turquoise about her throat . . . and she slipped out of her room and into the corridor.

There, she cannoned straight into Ralph Densham!

'Well, well! And who have we here?' he murmured appreciatively. His eyebrows rose a fraction. 'Well, if it isn't the country parson's daughter! Madam, you seem to be more elevated in position and wealth every time I meet you!' He reached out and fingered her borrowed necklace. 'From 'nothing worth stealing' to jewels fit for a lady!'

Katherine stepped back hastily, her fingers clutching the necklace.

'It is but borrowed, sir,' she excused herself. 'Your mother, Lady Densham . . . '

'Ah, yes! My mother! Has she taken you under her wing? It is one of her pleasures in life to take maidens in distress into her home and elevate them for a while.'

He leaned casually against the wall, effectively blocking her progress to the head of the stairs. His eyes studied her face, making her blush with embarrassment. 'So, you are the heroine I have heard talk of?'

He tipped up her face with a finger under her chin.

'Your beauty is but temporarily marred, Miss . . . Newcombe, is it not? Methinks I might still claim that kiss that you owe me!'

His mouth twisted into a semblance of a smile, though once again, it made Katherine shiver, not of fear. It was more like apprehension, a reading of his character that had a cruel twist to it.

'I think not, sir! I do not welcome your attention!' Her eyes flashed with anger. He had no right to speak to her thus!

The dinner gong rang once more, seizing both their attention.

Katherine drew herself tall. She stepped smartly past him to approach the stairway. Ralph's hand reached out and touched her shoulder.

'Your gown needs attention, Miss Newcombe. Allow me!'

Katherine could hear laughter in his voice but she obediently stood still. She had forgotten her unfastened buttons! How undignified!

On completing the task, Ralph turned her around to face him.

'Another service I have given you, Miss Newcombe! Do you still deny me my reward?'

He fingered the cravat at his neck, his dark eyes teasing upon her face.

Any remark Katherine might have made stuck in her throat. Her eyes were rivetted to the middle finger of Ralph's left hand.

A large green stone adorned his dress-ring. The gold fittings held it like two claws. She had seen such a ring a few weeks earlier — on the finger of one of the men in the coach that bore them from Honiton to Sidmouth.

A ring that had been stolen by the highwayman dressed in black . . .

Her mind registered the ring, his twisted smile, his dark cold eyes, and various phrases he had spoken that suddenly made sense. She had said the words, 'I have nothing worth stealing' at the scene of the robbery, and the highwayman had demanded a kiss!

She dropped her startled gaze and turned abruptly away from him, not wanting him to know her thoughts.

'A gentleman would not demand a reward for helping a lady!' she said breathlessly, beginning to descend the stairway. Her thoughts ran to the report that the highwayman had been shot . . . and Ralph Densham had been away for a few weeks. Recovering somewhere?

Her heart beat rapidly. She needed someone with whom to share this knowledge! And she could think of no-one but Miles. She would see him tomorrow evening. Could she hide her discovery from Ralph Densham until then?

Katherine didn't enjoy the evening.

Her sudden insight into Ralph's deception dominated her mind. As she listened to the conversations between the three Denshams, she couldn't help wondering if Lord and Lady Densham knew about their son's secret lifestyle and, if they did, how they felt about it.

'Is everything all right, Katherine?' Lady Densham enquired as the soup tureen was cleared away and replaced by a platter of roasted duck and dishes of lightly-steamed vegetables.

'Yes, thank you. I'm sorry to be so unsociable. I'm afraid I am concentrating on holding my cutlery without disgracing myself.' She laughed self-consciously. 'I feel all fingers and thumbs with these gloves on!' Which was partly true, she consoled herself, hating any form of deception.

Ralph seemed to be amused by her gaucheness, as if he were aware of her discovery but knew she had no option but to remain silent about it.

Soon after the two men had retired to do whatever men did after dinner,

Katherine also excused herself on the grounds of tiredness.

Sleep didn't come easily. Katherine turned all events over and over in her mind. Her new knowledge of the identity of the highwayman did not explain her other misgivings about the apparent wealth in the village and the events during the storm.

It was all beyond her and she had reached no conclusion that made sense when sleep finally overwhelmed her.

She had no difficulty evading Ralph the following day. He had left on business, Lady Densham informed her at lunchtime. Katherine paled slightly and glanced down at her plate. Were some more unfortunate travellers to be robbed of their valuables?

It was a fine, if chilly December afternoon and Katherine was strolling in the garden, leaving the hustle and bustle in the manor to the hordes of servants, all of whom seemed to know exactly what they were doing and what was needed where, when she heard shrieks of recognition and saw Henry, Zachary and Phoebe hurtling across the lawn towards her.

She ran towards them, her arms outstretched and stooped to hug them all at once.

'Katherine! Katherine! We've missed you!' Phoebe cried.

'And I've missed you!' Katherine assured them, tears springing to her eyes.

'Why are you wearing gloves?' Zachary asked curiously.

'I also hurt my hands. But they are almost better!' she added brightly, wishing to clear their anxious faces. 'Are your mamma and papa here?'

'Yes. Papa was taking Mamma inside. Shall we take you to them?' Phoebe offered, shyly slipping her hand into Katherine's. 'It doesn't hurt you to hold my hand, does it?'

'No, not now. It would have done a week ago. That's why I had to stay here, but I have longed to see you all again.'

Sarah received her joyfully, holding

out her arms to Katherine, who stooped down to receive a hug and even Reverend Burrows, normally more withdrawn than his wife, enveloped her briefly in his arms.

Sarah sighed with contentment. 'We will be back to being a family tomorrow, Katherine, dear.'

Miles' arrival was the next to bring her joy, although it was only two days since Katherine had last seen him. The weight of carrying in her mind the grave suspicions about Ralph Densham seemed to be lightened by his arrival, even though Katherine knew she would be unable to speak of it until they had some private moments together.

They met in the grand entrance hall under the crystal chandelier. Katherine was dressed in a pretty afternoon gown and her dark hair shone under the light of the chandelier.

Miles greeted her with warm formality, taking hold of her hand and bowing over it, taking her fingers to his lips.

'You look wonderful,' he admired. 'I

can see that this style of life becomes you! Will you miss it when you come back to us tomorrow?'

'No, I won't miss it. Everyone here has been very kind but it doesn't feel like home like it does at the vicarage.'

'Is that what you missed most? The vicarage?'

Katherine's cheeks flamed. Her hands were ungloved and she reached out and touched his face, wishing she could also let her fingers trail through his hair, and even pull down his face towards hers, and maybe he would kiss her.

Her thoughts went no further, though her lips tingled at the thought, remembering his kiss in the parlour at the inn. Or had she imagined that, along with everything else?

Miles took hold of the hand that had caressed his cheek and placed her palm against his lips.

As he took her hand away from his lips, he frowned as he saw the healing scars.

'Your poor hands,' he murmured,

taking hold of the other hand also. 'I hadn't realised the extent of their injury.' His frown deepened. 'It seems like rope-burn.'

'Yes. It was when I grabbed at the overhead rope over the raft. My arms were nearly pulled out of my sockets! I just knew I had to hold on!'

She spoke guilelessly, stating the simple facts of her remembrance of the event, temporarily forgetting the controversy about the occasion.

Miles glanced at her face and down to her hands again, his face serious. His thoughts were in conflict and, suddenly, he felt on the verge of something momentous. Katherine's tale had never varied and her present statement was completely without guile or rehearsal.

The healing scars bore out her version of events but, if that were so, it meant that everyone else connected with the incident had been lying — a conspiracy that involved almost the whole village!

9

At the top of the staircase, Ralph Densham surveyed the scene below. He drew in his breath sharply when he saw Katherine tenderly touching Miles' cheek and Miles kiss the palm of her hand. His dallying advances had been spurned because of a two-a-penny schoolmaster!

His lips curled into a twisted smile. He would soon sort that out!

The Christmas Ball was declared to be a great success by the entire village. Gifts of fruit and sugared confectionery were given to the children and hampers filled with enough succulent delights to ensure a hearty Christmas day meal for every family.

After a series of games, country dances and an appetising supper, the children were sent to the nursery to roll up in blankets and, though swearing to stay awake until dawn, they all eventually fell into a contented sleep.

The adults continued with their revelry . . . dancing or playing cards in an adjoining room, whichever took their fancy.

'Don't forget! I must speak with you soon!' Katherine reminded Miles as they parted at the end of the evening.

Miles, along with other single men and those couples who had no children asleep in the nursery, was to make his way home. There were enough guest-rooms to accommodate those who wished to stay overnight for whatever reason. No-one stood on ceremony and it was with much regret that the convivial gathering dispersed in the forenoon of Christmas Eve.

At the evening service at midnight, she exchanged fond glances with Miles above the heads of the older village children as they rendered their version of well-known carols, looking forward to his presence at the vicarage for Christmas dinner after morning service.

It was a crisp December day and Reverend Burrows and Sarah were happy to let their three older children walk in the woods with Katherine and Miles to run off their excesses at the past couple of days' hearty meals.

At last, Katherine was able to tell Miles of her astonishing realisation that none other than Ralph Densham was the highwayman who had been harrowing their county for the past two years or more.

Miles was, understandably, doubtful at first, though as Katherine recounted various conversations with him, and the references to her words spoken at the scene of the robbery, he had to acknowledge that it was a very rum do — especially when aligned to his suspicions about the cause of the injuries to Katherine's hands.

It was Henry who finally removed all his doubts when they came upon the raft that was pulled high up the bank and held fast by the rope tied around the trunk of a tree.

'Who's moved it?' he demanded indignantly, his hands on his hips.

'Moved it?' Katherine echoed, looking at the raft. 'Has it been moved?'

'Yes! See! It was fastened to this tree, under the rope!' Henry declared in no-nonsense fashion. 'Someone has moved it! You can't get hold of the rope from there!'

Miles looked at Katherine and back at the raft.

'He's right! It seems like I owe you an apology, my love.'

Katherine blushed slightly at his endearment. She felt that an enormous weight had fallen off her mind. Her memory wasn't playing tricks on her.

Her satisfied smile changed into a frown of perplexity.

'So, whom did I rescue? And where is he now? And why has everyone pretended that it didn't happen?'

Miles shook his head.

'I don't know, but I intend to find out!'

'So, what do we do, now?' she asked.

'I think we'd better tell Reverend Burrows, don't you?'

As soon as they were returned to the vicarage, they requested a private talk with Reverend Burrows.

He listened quietly as Miles told him of their discovery of the raft being moored to a different tree and the implications of that fact ... that it surely bore out Katherine's version of the rescue on the flooded river.

'Especially as the injuries to her hands look like rope burns,' he added.

Her hands were now much healed and it was now impossible to determine the cause of injury.

'We mustn't be too hasty here,' the reverend advised cautiously. 'This accusation involves leading members of the village, both in the act of secreting the man away and in the covering up of the deed afterwards. I agree that the moving of the raft seems to add weight to your suspicions but it is by no means conclusive. There could be a perfectly innocent reason for it to have been moved . . . to pull it farther up the bank, for one.'

'Yes, but there's more!' Katherine insisted.

Reverend Burrows' reaction to Katherine's disclosure about Ralph Densham was of evident disbelief.

'But he's a member of the aristocracy! He has no need to rob from the wealthy. Why should he put himself at risk in this manner?'

'For devilment, I'd say, sir!' Miles retorted. 'I suspect his life would otherwise be too stable for his liking.'

'I need time to consider what you've told me,' Reverend Burrows finally decided. 'I . . . er . . . know people who could possibly help to throw light upon the matter. In the meantime, I must ask you not to repeat any of this to anyone! Its announcement could lead to danger . . . to both of you!'

The remainder of the Christmas

season passed in comparative peace and it was late in the afternoon of the day before the school was due to reopen that Miles appeared on the vicarage doorstep, his usual equanimity replaced by puzzled anger.

'My terms of employment have been withdrawn!' he announced bitterly, without preamble. 'It seems there is someone in this village who wants to be rid of me!'

Katherine's face fell in shock and dismay.

'But, why? Who?'

'I don't know! But I intend to find out! Is Reverend Burrows at home?'

'Why, yes. He's in his study preparing his sermon for Sunday.'

He brandished a letter at her while saying, 'It says in here that I have failed to come up to the standard required by the board of authority, and Reverend Burrows is the head of that board!'

'But that doesn't make sense! Both he and Sarah have often sung your praises!'

'Then he has obviously changed his mind — or had it changed for him! Who is the most influential person in this village?'

Katherine pursed her lips. 'Lord Densham, I suppose.'

'Exactly! The father of Ralph Densham . . . our friend, the highwayman.'

Katherine waited anxiously whilst Miles went in to speak with Reverend Burrows. She heard raised voices and feared that all was not going well. When Miles emerged, his face was like thunder.

'He says he can do nothing for me! The decision was taken out of his hands,' Miles exclaimed. 'The parents don't like my leniency! Nor my new way of doing things!'

'That's not true. You make school enjoyable! What will you do? Where will you go? Your house . . . ?'

'Goes with the job! I have to vacate it tomorrow!'

'Oh, no!' Katherine felt distraught. Her thoughts became more personal.

'What about . . . us?' she queried softly.

Miles took her in his arms and buried his face in her hair.

'Don't worry! I'll think of something!' He laughed shakily.

'But why has it happened? Why now?' She pulled away from him slightly so that she look at him directly.

'I can't help thinking it has something to do with what we have discovered . . . but we've only . . . ' She glanced towards the closed study door.

'Precisely! We haven't told anyone else.'

He glanced about them carefully, not wanting anyone to overhear.

'Come and see me off,' he said quietly, drawing her outside with him.

When they reached the gate, he put his hands on her shoulders and smiled into her eyes.

'I won't be going far. I can manage without getting a job for a few weeks, and, with no job to go to, I can spend time investigating things.'

Katherine glanced back towards the

vicarage, shocked to realise the implications. But Reverend Burrows was a man of the church . . . above reproach, as her father had been.

Miles faced her seriously.

'I have to go! But don't worry. They aren't going to get away with whatever it is that's going on! Now, listen carefully. Don't do anything to upset anyone or make anyone think you are suspicious about anything.

'And, as soon as I get somewhere to stay, I'll find a way to let you know where I am. But you mustn't tell anyone.'

Katherine nodded and huddled against him, not wanting to let go of him.

Miles tipped up her chin and kissed her with an urgency she hadn't known before . . . and then he was gone.

Sarah knew about Miles' dismissal and offered sympathy and platitudes to Katherine. Not knowing how far she could trust Sarah, Katherine said little and her distress was genuine.

The school children were naturally

upset at their teacher's sudden departure and were simply told that Mr Westcott had left and Reverend Burrows would teach them until a new master was appointed.

It was late afternoon the following Monday when, after settling Grace down for her afternoon nap because her mamma was indisposed with a headache, that Katherine went in search of the other children, intending to take them to the village shop to spend some of their Christmas pennies. She found Phoebe drawing in the nursery but of Henry and Zachary there was no sign.

Phoebe seemed reluctant to speak of them, but, when pressed, she put down her crayon and folded her arms, a look of resignation upon her face.

'I told them not to go!' she declared self-righteously. 'They will be in serious trouble with Papa when he comes home, you just see!'

Katherine felt her heart begin to race with trepidation. She controlled her voice and asked quite calmly, 'Where have they gone, Phoebe?'

'They told me not to tell!'

'Sometimes, it's right to tell, Phoebe. For instance, do you think that it could be dangerous, this place they've gone to?'

Phoebe considered the question. She pressed her lips together and nodded.

'They've gone up on the moors looking for smugglers.'

10

Katherine's hands flew to her chest, her fingers spread across her fast-beating heart.

'How long have they been gone? Do you know?'

'Since straight after lunch.'

Katherine thought quickly. Reverend Burrows was out visiting an elderly parishioner and Sarah was sleeping soundly. She was reluctant to waken her with such a worry so she decided to confide in Alice and leave her in charge of Phoebe and Grace.

'Martha, will you run to the village and ask for any of the men who are around to follow me up there?'

She knew that the cottage where Miles was staying wasn't far off her route but, when she called there, he wasn't at home.

'He's due back on the next stagecoach

from Exeter, m'dearie,' his landlady told her.

Surely the boys couldn't be too far ahead of her! She scrambled up the steep woodland path through the plantation of trees. The path diverged after a while and, after a moment's reflection, she chose the steeper one as being the most likely to lead to the moor.

A layer of cloud now obscured the wintry sun of noonday and it was getting thicker by the minute. The light was fading fast. Katherine hurried on, pausing every few minutes to call the boys' names.

'Henry! Zachary! Where are you?'

But there was no answer.

Swirls of mist were beginning to snake their way over the low-lying bushes, causing a rush of anxiety.

She changed direction again and hurried on. Reaching a rise, she paused and swung her gaze all around. She thought she heard the neighing of a horse or pony and stopped again, trying to determine its direction.

'Henry! Zachary! Over here!'

'Katherine!' She heard Henry's voice call.

Katherine whirled around and peered through the wraiths of white mist.

As two small figures emerged from the mist a pistol shot rang out! Katherine flung herself on to the boys, pushing them to the ground.

'Lie still!' Katherine commanded them.

She heard hoof beats approaching and a sturdy pony loomed above them. She struggled to rise but a rough masculine voice commanded, 'Stay where you are!'

More men and ponies appeared, forming a circle around Katherine and the boys. They weren't villagers, that was for sure. Katherine felt alarmed by their appearance and more so by the belligerent expressions on their faces.

'Are they the smugglers?' Zachary asked in a matter-of-fact way.

Katherine attempted to laugh, though

she felt anything but amused.

'Of course not!' she said lightly. 'I expect they have come up here to help to search for you, as I have.' She twisted round to face the first man who had appeared. 'Am I right?' she asked. 'Are you part of the search party out looking for these two scallywags who have heard too many stories about smugglers than is good for them? Gave us all a scare, they did, I can tell you!' she added.

Katherine could sense that the group of men had relaxed a little, though none of them seeming willing to be the first to break their silence. She was almost convinced that they were indeed part of a smuggling gang, though the packs on the ponies' backs were empty of contraband.

She raised herself into a sitting position, hoping her smile looked more genuine than it felt.

'May we get up now, please? The boys have learned their lesson, I think, and their father, Reverend Burrows of

Ottersleigh, will be anxious to know they are safe and well.'

'Ah . . . I suppose so. Reverend Burrows, you say. That makes it all right then, don't it? We be heading that way, miss.' He turned to the others. 'Lift the boys on to two ponies and we'll be on our way! What about you, miss? Do you want to ride or walk?'

Katherine began to feel easier in her mind. The men seemed to accept their tale, whatever their purpose was in being here.

'I'll walk, thank you. I've never ridden and the way down will be quite steep,' she replied pleasantly.

The boys were lifted on to two ponies and their high spirits seemed to return. Katherine concentrated on keeping up a spate of light chatter with the boys to allay their anxiety.

When they reached the lane that would lead straight down into the village, the men leading the boys' ponies had already crossed the lane and were descending down towards the river.

Too late did she see the large rowing boat at that very moment being steered towards the bank and recognised Nick Conybear as being the man who had caught the rope thrown from the boat to enable it to be tied fast. And wasn't that Jacob Gillard, the innkeeper, farther along?

'Come on, Jack! You're running late!' Nick called over his shoulder.

With a sharp intake of breath, Katherine betrayed the fact that she understood the significance of Nick's words. She strove to recover the situation by saying brightly, 'Well, we'll be on our way now. Thank you kindly for your help! Come on, Henry, Zachary! Say goodbye to the kind men and let's be off home. Your mamma will be quite anxious!'

'What the devil!' she heard Nick exclaim. 'What are they doing here, man?'

Katherine could see guilt and anger

on their faces . . . and fear of discovery. She wanted to assure them that she wouldn't say anything to anyone, if only they'd let the boys go . . . but she wasn't sure how true that was and the words stuck in her throat.

Angry shouts from the other men on the boat and on the riverbank erupted and the men who had brought them down off the moor belatedly realised their error.

Katherine turned to Nick Conybear.

'The children were lost on the moor. These men brought us down. They might have died up there in the mist.'

'Aye, and what d'you think might happen to 'em here?' he asked brusquely.

'You must let them go! They don't realise what is happening. They have talked of smugglers for the past month or so.'

'Aye, since that meddling schoolmaster began to poke is nose in!'

'Please don't frighten them! I tell you, they will do you no harm!'

'How do we know we can trust them? Or you?'

Katherine sensed he was wavering in their favour . . . but another man called out, 'Tie 'em up! How long do ye think any of 'em will keep their mouth shut?'

'But they're only lads! The vicar's lads! He's one of us! He'll make sure it goes no further,' Nick tried to convince the others.

'And what about her?' one man asked, nodding in Katherine's direction. 'What will they make of her ramblings?'

Nick glanced at her briefly.

'That's all they'll think it is, rambling! She's had a bang on her head and her mind's not clear. No-one gives credit to her tales.'

'We can't risk it! Tie her up and put her in the boat. We'll dump her at sea — and take those lads back on to the moor and lose them there!'

Katherine lay on the bottom of the boat, her limbs sore and cramped. A length of cloth tied in her mouth made breathing difficult and calling out

166

impossible. But what about Henry and Zachary? Were they to be left to die?

The creaking of oars in rowlocks sounded. She heard exclamations of anger and a man's impatient voice saying, 'Let me see her?'

She heard him draw in his breath sharply . . . and then, 'Turn this way, missie!'

Something in his voice made her respond, and she found herself staring at the man whom she had rescued from the river nearly a month earlier. He clambered over the side and into the boat and pulled out his cutlass.

Katherine blanched. Was he going to dispatch her swiftly in recompense for saving him? She instinctively flinched and tried to roll away but when the knife fell, it sliced through her bonds, not her flesh.

'What yer doing, Sam? She'll blab to the excise men!'

'She saved my life — now I've saved hers. Sam Mutter pays his debts!'

He helped her to her feet and over the side. She stumbled but he held her steady.

'All I ask is twenty-four hours, miss!' His eyes held hers. 'We'll clear everything out. There'll be nothing left to prove your tale.'

'Make the boys think it's all been a game,' Katherine said to him. 'They might have bad dreams for a few nights but then they'll forget.'

He shook her hand and nodded, then let out a jovial laugh and approached the terrified boys, who were tied together seated on the ground.

'Ho-ho, me hearties! That was a good game, wasn't it? Had enough of smuggling now, have 'ee? Ye won't be going up on that moor on your own again, will ye? Shiver me timbers!'

Henry and Zachary shook their heads, wide-eyed with fright. Once untied, they boys stumbled over to Katherine, who hugged them tightly.

'There! That was a fine game, wasn't it, boys?' she said brightly, her voice trembling. 'They really had me worried for a minute!'

'I wasn't scared!' Henry boasted,

though his voice wavered slightly.

The men at the riverside were hastily loading up the packhorses and leading them back up through the trees and the first boat was already pushed back into mid-river.

Katherine had a hand on both boys' shoulders.

'Come on! It's time to go home.'

They turned, only to step back again in alarm. The black-clad figure of Ralph Densham towered over them on his black stallion.

'A touching scene!' he drawled. 'The man's going soft since his ducking in the river. I think you should have left him there, m'dear! I demand a higher price than twenty-four hours of silence for your freedom, Miss Newcombe!'

Katherine glanced nervously to the men at the water's edge but all were too busy unloading and loading to notice this extra drama.

'Sam Mutter has set us free!' she declared. 'Who are you to go against his order?'

Ralph reached out with his folded riding whip and tilted up Katherine's face with it.

'No man tells me what to do! Nor woman!' he added, his cold smile twisting his face. 'You haven't asked me my price! But no matter, I will tell you! You are my price, Miss Newcombe.'

He laughed as she flinched and stepped backwards, taking the boys with her . . . and he urged his horse forward step by step with her, his whip still flicking under her chin.

'I may even marry you . . . if you please me! That would guarantee your silence! Did you know that a wife cannot turn King's evidence against her husband, Miss Newcombe?'

'Stop!'

The harsh challenge seemed to echo, coming from the river and from the track up to the vicarage simultaneously.

'Miles!'

He had emerged from the trees and stood at the end of the track. Even as Katherine saw him and called his name, he began to advance.

Ralph laughed and backed his horse a few steps, superbly controlling its mettlesome spirit. He drew a pistol from his belt, levelling it at Miles.

Miles moved sideways, forcing Ralph to turn his horse away from Katherine and the boys.

'Run to the vicarage, boys! And you, Katherine!' Miles said quietly.

'Stay where you are!' Ralph commanded them. 'Or I shoot your friend.'

He fired his pistol into the air.

'Get down off your horse and face me on equal terms, like a man!' Miles challenged, recklessly striding forwards, hand outstretched to grasp the horse's bridle.

'You fool! Get out of my way!' Ralph snarled.

He had drawn his second pistol and now levelled it at Miles.

Katherine could see the glint in his eyes and knew he was going to shoot.

'No!' she screamed, running forward . . . as a shot rang out!

11

Katherine expected to see Miles crumbling to the ground before she reached him, but he didn't. It was Ralph Densham who fell backwards off his horse, in slow motion it seemed. Then, the horse bolted, dragging Ralph's body still attached to one stirrup by his riding boot.

Ashen-faced, Katherine clung to Miles and began to beat his chest with her fists.

'You stupid, stupid man! You could have been killed!'

Miles took hold of the hands that were about to pummel him once more.

'I know — but I was determined you wouldn't!'

They looked over her head to where Sam Mutter was standing motionless.

'And no man countermands Sam Mutter!' Sam said flatly, pushing his spent pistol back into his belt. 'Be off with you! We'll clear up here.'

Dazed, Katherine allowed Miles to hustle her up the track to where Henry and Zachary were standing, white-faced.

When they arrived at the vicarage, it seemed as though half the villagers were there, obviously about to set off in search of them.

Sarah tearfully held out her arms to them and Katherine pushed the boys towards hers.

With a cry of, 'Mamma!' they ran to her.

Their father strode over to them, not knowing whether to be angry with them or relieved that they were safe.

'They need a hot bath and to be put to bed,' Katherine suggested, anxious to get them upstairs away from everyone before they spoke of what had happened, determined to give Sam Mutter his twenty-four hours of silence.

The strength then seemed to drain out of Katherine and she looked helplessly at Miles.

'I feel rather faint,' she breathed softly, and promptly slid to the ground.

When she came to, she was lying on the sofa in Sarah's parlour. Miles was kneeling at her side, holding a cold flannel to her forehead.

Sarah was in her wheelchair, looking on anxiously and Reverend Burrows looked white with shock. Katherine guessed that Miles had told him as much as he knew about the events.

'I think a sip of brandy might be beneficial,' Sarah suggested. 'I know you don't drink alcohol, Katherine, but it is known to be very therapeutic in such circumstances.'

In stops and starts, with many pauses whilst she cleared her mind, she eventually told them everything that had happened and everything that had been said.

Reverend Burrows sank his head into his hands.

'I am much to blame,' he admitted. 'I'm sorry, Sarah. I knew you wouldn't like it but it seemed the only way to manage after your accident.'

He looked apologetically at Katherine and Miles.

'One night, nearly two years ago now, I was out, giving communion to a dying man. Sarah was near to her time with Grace and, unable to sleep, she saw lights outside and, careless of her own safety, she put on a cloak and went outside. The lights were then in the church and she went to investigate, thinking someone was in need of help. It was some villagers, storing contraband goods in the crypt. Apparently, it had gone on for years, always on occasions when I was called away, sometimes falsely, I later discovered.'

He looked at his wife and took hold of her hand, stroking it tenderly.

'The men realised they were discovered and rushed out, carelessly knocking Sarah aside in their haste. She fell down the chancel steps, landing hard upon the concrete floor. When the men realised who it was who had disturbed them, some returned and carried her back into the vicarage. She went into labour and Grace was born, a few weeks early but she was healthy and suffered no harm. However, that wasn't the case with Sarah. The fall had damaged her back and she has never walked since.'

He held Sarah to him for a moment, as he relived those difficult days. This time, it was Sarah who patted his hand as she looked up adoringly at him.

'And you have cared for me as no other husband has ever cared for his wife!' she assured him gently.

His shoulders sagged and it seemed as though he wouldn't continue but he visibly pulled himself together and went on.

'We had to have so much help, I knew I couldn't afford it. Some of the men came to me. They admitted what had happened, and came up with a plan. They would supply us with all that we needed in return for letting them continue to use the church crypt to hide their illegal goods.

'I was weak. They convinced me that no-one was being robbed. The goods were paid for in their country of origin. All they were doing was avoiding paying the government tax. When they told me how many of the villagers were involved I was astounded. Very few were outside of the co-operative group. After some days of thought and prayer, I agreed to their suggestion. All I told Sarah was that people were giving more of their tithes.'

He looked at Sarah. 'Can you forgive me for deceiving you?' he asked. 'When I think how it nearly caused the death of our two boys, I know I am asking a lot of you!'

Sarah looked at him sadly.

'Of course I forgive you! You did what you thought was best . . . but, what are we to do now? How can we continue to live like this when we now know what might have happened?'

'We can't!' Reverend Burrows' tone made his position clear. 'Those smuggling contraband into the country become desperate men when faced with discovery. Yet how can I betray them to the authorities without implicating ourselves? And if I were to confess my part, what would become of you and our children, Sarah?'

Miles reached for Katherine's hand.

'My decision is easier to make. I am already dismissed from my post. If Katherine . . .'

'That was Ralph Densham's doing,' Reverend Burrows interrupted. 'He threatened retribution if you were not dismissed. The majority of villagers were intimidated into agreeing.'

'Did they know he was the highwayman?' Miles asked.

'Yes. It was a matter, of 'I'll not tell on you, if you don't tell on me!' Ben Gillard often acts as courier between the two factions.'

Katherine sighed. 'Lord and Lady Densham, how much are they involved?'

'Up to the hilt!' Reverend Burrows declared. 'And others, far too many to mention.'

Katherine pressed her lips together.

'I cannot stay here in this village! I trusted these people. I don't know where I shall go, but I cannot condone what has gone on!'

Reverend Burrows hung his head.

'You put me to shame, my dear! I should have stood against it from the time I first knew of it. I put self-interest first.'

'Might I make a suggestion?' Miles asked.

'Of course.'

'We cannot change a whole village,' Miles began reasonably. 'Sam Mutter asked for twenty-four hours' silence. Because he went against the others and saved the lives of Katherine and the children, I feel we must give him that. Then, I suggest that I report my misgivings about the comings and goings that I noticed. The villagers have already thrown me out. I doubt they'll do more. When the authorities come to make a search, they probably won't find anything but it might make the villagers have second thoughts about starting up again.'

He smiled faintly at Reverend Burrows and Sarah.

'That leaves you free to take your time making whatever decisions you feel are right for you and your family, doesn't it?'

Sarah nodded, looking hopefully at her husband.

'We could ask the bishop to look out for a suitable living for us elsewhere, couldn't we?' She clasped hold of his hand. 'We owe it to the children to rear them in a safe environment, George. Don't you agree? And what about you, Katherine, dear? Will you feel able to stay with us until we are offered a new living? I sincerely hope so!'

'Yes, that is . . . ' Katherine stopped. She knew Miles cared for her, but now he had neither a position nor a home. He would need time.

Miles understood her predicament. He took hold of her hand and lifted it to his lips. His eyes smiled at her as his lips caressed the backs of her fingers.

Katherine's lips parted breathlessly as she read the message in his eyes and her cheeks felt warm.

'I know we haven't known each other for very long,' Miles began. 'I love you, Katherine!'

He gallantly dropped to one knee, still holding her hand and gazing at her with fervent devotion.

'Will you marry me, Katherine? I know that at the moment, I have no means of supporting you, but I am confident that I won't be in this position for very long. I'm sure of that.'

'Yes, I will,' Katherine declared, unable to hold back her answer until he had finished. 'I love you, too!'

'Oh, George! Isn't that lovely!' Sarah exclaimed happily. 'A wedding in the family! Oh, you will let George marry you, won't you?'

But, neither of them heard her. They were too busy sealing their betrothal with a kiss.

We do hope that you have enjoyed reading this large print book.

Did you know that all of our titles are available for purchase?

We publish a wide range of high quality large print books including:
Romances, Mysteries, Classics
General Fiction
Non Fiction and Westerns

Special interest titles available in large print are:
The Little Oxford Dictionary
Music Book, Song Book
Hymn Book, Service Book

Also available from us courtesy of Oxford University Press:
Young Readers' Dictionary
(large print edition)
Young Readers' Thesaurus
(large print edition)

For further information or a free brochure, please contact us at:
Ulverscroft Large Print Books Ltd.,
The Green, Bradgate Road, Anstey,
Leicester, LE7 7FU, England.
Tel: (00 44) **0116 236 4325**
Fax: (00 44) **0116 234 0205**

Other titles in the
Linford Romance Library:

DANGER COMES CALLING

Karen Abbott –

Elaine Driscoe and her sister Kate expect their walking holiday along Offa's Dyke Path to be a peaceful pursuit — until a chance encounter with a mysterious stranger casts a shadow of fear over everything. Their steps are constantly crossed by three men — Niall, Steve and Phil. But which of them can they trust? And what is the ultimate danger that awaits them in Prestatyn?

NO SUBSTITUTE FOR LOVE

Dina McCall

Although recently made redundant, nurse Holly Fraser decides to spend some of her savings on a Christmas coach tour in Scotland. When the tour reaches the Callender Hotel, several people mistake Holly for a Mrs MacEwan. Furthermore, Ian MacEwan arrives to take her to the Hall, convinced that she is his wife, Carol! Although Ian despises Carol for having deserted him and their two small children, two-year-old Lucy needs her mother. Holly stays to help the child, but finds herself in an impossible situation.

LOVE'S SWEET SECRETS

Bridget Thorn

When her parents die, Melanie comes home to run their guest house and to try to win the Jubilee Prize for her father's garden. But her sister, Angela, wants her to sell the property, and her boyfriend, Michael, wants a partnership and marriage. Just before the Spring opening, Paul Hunt arrives and helps Melanie when the garden is attacked by vandals. After the news is splashed over the national papers, guests cancel. Then real danger threatens. But who is the enemy?

OUT OF THE SHADOWS

Judy Chard

Why does Carol Marsh, the new receptionist at the country inn in Devon, have to report to the police regularly? Why does she never ask for time off and rejects all attempts by the owner, Norman Willis, to be friendly? Then, Norman's wife is found dead in suspicious circumstances. Could Carol have had some part in her death? Yvonne's relationship with her husband had deteriorated since Carol's arrival. Maybe Carol and Norman have a deeper, more sinister relationship than that of employer and employee.